AROUND CHI-TOWN

Add Tara Connelly Paige to the list of Connellys having troubles of late. Seems the comely heiress has been getting crank calls and has been followed. The incidents spooked her enough for her father, Grant, to beef up security on the Connelly clan.

But even more bizarre is the "resurrection" of her "deceased" husband, Michael Paige. According to our sources, after being missing and presumed dead for two long years, Michael calmly opened the door of the family's Lake Shore Manor as if returning from a long day at the office. "Honey, I'm home"? Not.

In a turn of events straight out of a soap opera, Michael had never been on that train that crashed in Ecuador, but instead met with foul play that left him with amnesia. Finally, two weeks ago, he regained his memory and has just returned to Chicago. Certainly truth *is* stranger than fiction!

No telling how Grant Connelly will react to his long-lost son-in-law's return. The proverbial bad boy from the wrong side of the tracks, Michael had once stolen away "Daddy's little girl" for a hasty elopement. And it's no secret that the Connelly patriarch had new plans for Tara that didn't include Michael.

Tune in for more details as they break....

Dear Reader,

Welcome to Silhouette Desire! This month we've created a brand-new lineup of passionate, powerful and provocative love stories just for you.

Begin your reading enjoyment with *Ride the Thunder* by Lindsay McKenna, the September MAN OF THE MONTH and the second book in this beloved author's cross-line series, MORGAN'S MERCENARIES: ULTIMATE RESCUE. An amnesiac husband recovers his memory and returns to his wife and child in *The Secret Baby Bond* by Cindy Gerard, the ninth title in our compelling DYNASTIES: THE CONNELLYS continuity series.

Watch a feisty beauty fall for a wealthy lawman in *The Sheriff & the Amnesiac* by Ryanne Corey. Then meet the next generation of MacAllisters in *Plain Jane MacAllister* by Joan Elliott Pickart, the newest title in THE BABY BET: MACALLISTER'S GIFTS.

A night of passion leads to a marriage of convenience between a gutsy heiress and a macho rodeo cowboy in *Expecting Brand's Baby*, by debut Desire author Emilie Rose. And in Katherine Garbera's new title, *The Tycoon's Lady* falls off the stage into his arms at a bachelorette auction, as part of our popular BRIDAL BID theme promotion.

Savor all six of these sensational new romances from Silhouette Desire today.

Enjoy!

Joan Marlow Golan

Joan Marlow Golan
Senior Editor, Silhouette Desire

Please address questions and book requests to:
Silhouette Reader Service
U.S.: 3010 Walden Ave., P.O. Box 1325, Buffalo, NY 14269
Canadian: P.O. Box 609, Fort Erie, Ont. L2A 5X3

The Secret
Baby Bond
CINDY GERARD

Silhouette® Desire®

Published by Silhouette Books

America's Publisher of Contemporary Romance

Special thanks and acknowledgment are given to Cindy Gerard for her contribution to the DYNASTIES: THE CONNELLYS series.

This book is dedicated to the intrepid authors who participated in the writing of this wonderful series of books. Ladies, it was a pleasure.

 SILHOUETTE BOOKS

ISBN 0-373-76460-X

THE SECRET BABY BOND

Visit Silhouette at www.eHarlequin.com

Printed in U.S.A.

Books by Cindy Gerard

Silhouette Desire

The Cowboy Takes a Lady #957
Lucas: The Loner #975
*The Bride Wore Blue #1012
*A Bride for Abel Greene #1052
*A Bride for Crimson Falls #1076
†The Outlaw's Wife #1175
†Marriage, Outlaw Style #1185
†The Outlaw Jesse James #1198
Lone Star Prince #1256
In His Loving Arms #1293
Lone Star Knight #1353
The Bridal Arrangement #1392
The Secret Baby Bond #1460

*Northern Lights Brides
†Outlaw Hearts

CINDY GERARD

If asked "What's your idea of heaven?" Cindy Gerard would say a warm sun, a cool breeze, pan pizza and a good book. If she had to settle for one of the four, she'd opt for the book, with the pizza running a close second. Inspired by the pleasure she's received from the books she's read and her longtime love affair with her husband, Tom, Cindy now creates her own evocative and sensual love stories about compelling characters and complex relationships.

This bestselling author of close to twenty books has received numerous industry awards, among them the National Readers' Choice Award, multiple *Romantic Times* nominations and two RITA® Award nominations from the Romance Writers of America. Cindy loves to hear from her readers and invites them to visit her Web page at www.tlt.com/authors/cgerard.htm.

MEET THE CONNELLYS

Meet the Connellys of Chicago—
wealthy, powerful and rocked by scandal,
betrayal...and passion!

Who's Who in
THE SECRET BABY BOND

Michael Paige—He'd spent two years in an Ecuadorian jungle, not knowing who he was, until a twist of fate gave him back his memory and luck gave him a way home....

Tara Connelly Paige—Sex was never the problem between her and Michael; communication was. But at the sight of her husband, she's the one who's speechless....

Ruby—This unflappable manager of Lake Shore Manor has served the Connellys for thirty-five years. There are few things she *hasn't* seen....

Prologue

For two years, Michael Paige had been a dead man. To some, he was a dead man still. In actuality, not only was he alive, he finally remembered the many things that he'd forgotten.

He remembered what he'd had.

He remembered what he'd lost.

And he wanted it back.

From a distance, from behind dark glasses, he watched Tara—the wife he'd lost even before the world had decided he was dead—while his wildly beating heart reminded him how very much alive he truly was.

Sitting quietly on the park bench, while the early September sun shined brilliant and pure through the shifting oaks and the scent of summer's last roses drifted on the breeze, he watched. And he remembered the way she moved, the way her short, sleek cap of stylish black hair felt sliding like silk between his fingers, the way her violet eyes clouded to misty lavender when he made love to her. Two years ago. A lifetime ago.

She smiled, her face full of love for the child who toddled by her side. The boy wore tiny running shoes, a baby-sized Chicago Cubs jacket and cap and stared up at his mother through laughing gray eyes.

Through *his* eyes.

A lump formed in his throat that he couldn't swallow. *He had a son.*

He had a son whose name was Brandon, whose face he'd seen and whose name he'd learned for the first time just two weeks ago. Michael buried his hand in his jacket pocket and clutched the dog-eared piece of newsprint. The photo of Tara in the grainy gray print of a tabloid newspaper had caught his eye in a Quito, Ecuador supermarket and blindsided him with a staggering rush of memory. So had the dramatic account of his own death.

A shooting pain stabbed through his right temple. He touched two fingers to the scar there and rode it out. It would pass soon and until it did, he focused on reality.

The reality of his wife. The reality of his son.

An ache swelled and grew and filled his chest with a love and a longing so profound that he almost went to the boy then. Just to gather him close. To feel that robust and healthy little body warm and real against his own. To look into his liquid silver eyes and see a reflection of himself there. To cement into fact that the amazing miracle he and Tara had made together was not a cruel trick of his imagination. And to confirm, unequivocally, that he really was alive.

But the man who had been Miguel Santiago for the past two years couldn't do that. Not yet. Not here. So he stayed where he was and accepted that this was not the time. This was not the way. He couldn't just walk up to his child—his child who didn't know him. He couldn't just smile and say to his wife, "I'm not dead. I was just lost for a while. And I've missed you."

He couldn't say any of those things because to Tara, he was dead. And because, just before he died, she'd told him she wanted a divorce.

So he sat, unable to move, unwilling to leave as his son tumbled to his back with a shriek of gurgling laughter—and the man at Tara's side bent to pick him up and lift him into his arms.

Then the three of them walked away together. Tara, his son and the man who would take his place—or so said the tabloids.

It was only after they'd faded to a memory that he realized his hands were clenched into fists inside his pockets, that his eyes were staring blankly.

"Mister... Hey, mister, you okay?"

He looked up abruptly, squinted against the crisp September sun. A tall, gangly teenager frowned down at him. The boy had a basketball tucked under his arm and freckles bridging his nose. He wore baggy pants, a sloppy Chicago Bulls T-shirt and an expression that mixed wariness with concern. Even from where he stood, a cautious couple of yards away, Michael could smell the salt and sweat and vitality of him.

"Man," the kid said. "You're white as a ghost."

A ghost.

It should have been funny.

If the kid only knew.

Michael took one last look at the spot where his wife and son had disappeared. Then he rose and started walking.

This time he promised himself that when he walked,

it would be out of the shadows. This time he would walk toward the living, not away.

He wanted his life back.

He wanted his wife back.

He did not want to be dead any longer.

One

Tara Connelly Paige sat cross-legged on the plush rose carpet that covered the floor in the den at Lake Shore Manor. She stared into a fire that cut the unusual chill of the early September evening.

Beside her, on his favorite quilt that was soft and blue and plump with the loving care his great-grandmother, Nana Lilly Connelly had sewn into it, fourteen-month-old Brandon slept like the babe he was: blissful, innocent, ignorant of the turmoil his mother was feeling.

"It's a little late for second thoughts, Tara," her father said carefully from the sofa behind her.

Tara looked up and over her shoulder into the concern in Grant Connelly's eyes. It shouldn't surprise her anymore that her father could read her thoughts. His insight was almost frightening. He didn't call it insight, though. He called it understanding.

Maybe he was right. It seemed that since she'd

moved back home to Lake Shore Manor after Michael
died two years ago, her father could read her mind almost as well as he read the market. It was another reason that it was past time for her to move back out on
her own—or move in with John.

Move in with John.

Too much reluctance accompanied the possibility.
With reluctance came guilt.

"I know it was a hard decision, honey, but John is
right," her father continued. "And you're right to finally have Seth initiate the legal work to have Michael
declared legally dead."

Michael. Dead.

She drew in a serrated breath. Tried, as she always
tried, to let go of the hope that after all this time he
could be alive. Intellectually, she knew it wasn't possible. If her intellect wasn't enough, her family's gentle
but insistent persuasion was. Even Seth had finally
jumped on the wagon.

Thank God for Seth. Her brother, the lawyer. Her
brother who had morphed Tara into Terror when they
were kids and whom she loved to tease—or at least she
had once loved to tease him.

*"Hey, Seth, what do you call five hundred lawyers at
the bottom of the ocean?"*

*"I'll bite, brat. What do you call five hundred lawyers
at the bottom of the ocean?"*

"A good start."

A small smile lifted one corner of her mouth then
quickly dropped away. She hadn't seen much of Seth's
flashing grin lately. But then again, he hadn't seen much
of hers, either.

He was there for her, though, as the rest of her brothers and sisters had always been there for her. Seth was

handling the paperwork it had taken her two years to gather the courage to set in motion. Smoothly, efficiently, discreetly. Seth was a man you could count on. Much like their father.

Tara looked at him. At sixty-five, Grant Connelly was still a handsome man. His granite jaw was a perfect complement to his deep tan and dark hair, but it was his eyes that set him apart. One quelling look from Connelly Corporation CEO's steel gray eyes and grown men cowered, women wept.

She'd been the benefactor of those looks herself, though not for a while. Definitely not tonight. Tonight his eyes were gentle, as they always were for his wife and for his children. When Brandon snuffled in his sleep and tucked his chubby little fist under his chin with a sigh of baby ecstasy, steel-gray transitioned to an indulgent, smoky silver.

They shared a smile then for this precious child whose power ran the gamut from melting hearts with his laughter or his tears, to raising roofs when he was full of himself and wanting everyone's attention. Out of the softness of her father's smile came more concern.

"The boy needs a father, Tara."

She swallowed, looked at her hands and agreed softly. "I know."

"John wants to be his father. He wants to be your husband. He's a good man, honey."

Yes, John was a good man. A little stuffy, per Seth, but good. Good for Brandon. Good for her. He gave her direction, offered security, even the extravagant lifestyle she was accustomed to. The opportunity to move back out from under her parents' roof. She'd taken advantage of their indulgence long enough.

John offered all the answers, provided all the solutions—all but one. She didn't love him. Not that way. Not the way she'd loved Michael.

The fire crackled. She looked from the blue/yellow flame to her left hand and the two-carat diamond solitaire John had given her three weeks ago. Firelight glinted off the brilliant and perfectly faceted marquise. She thought of the inexpensive, plain gold band Michael had given her, remembered the love and the hopes and the dreams he'd offered with it.

Love, however, hadn't solved the problems they'd amassed during their turbulent five years together. Love hadn't been the be-all or end-all to everything that had gone wrong between them. For that reason, it didn't seem essential for love to factor in to her relationship with John. She cared for him, as much, she thought, as he cared for her. In the end, it seemed reason enough to finally agree to marry him.

"So," her father persisted as he lifted the one scotch he allowed himself every evening. Ice shifted, clinked softly in the Waterford crystal glass. "Are you close to setting a wedding date?"

She let out a deep breath. Like her father, John had also been pressing her to set a date. She'd been dragging her feet ever since the story had been picked up by every legitimate and illegitimate news publication in the country. The public announcement of their engagement two weeks ago had seemed like an act of betrayal. It also seemed so final.

She rubbed a finger across her brow, unable to ignore the dull headache pounding there. She hadn't been prepared for the media circus the announcement had become. The tabloids had taken cannibalistic delight in catching pictures of her and John together, pictures of Brandon.

The worst, though, was the resurrection of the photographs of the train wreck in Ecuador that had claimed Michael's life. Reliving the sensationalized and gruesome accounts of Michael's disappearance had been a nightmare. Because of it, she hadn't been able to think about setting a wedding date with John. For reasons she didn't fully understand, she hadn't wanted to.

"It's a little early for definite plans considering..."

Grant frowned at his drink, then at his daughter when her words trailed off.

"Considering that you've never gotten over Michael."

She folded a corner of the quilt over Brandon's little body. The flannel felt soft and real beneath her fingers. Very few things felt real lately. She scooted back until her shoulders rested against the sofa.

"I was over him before he died," she said, trying to make them both believe it.

"And yet..." Grant covered her slim shoulder with his hand. She was his little girl and she was hurting. "And yet it hurts you to think of his death as an absolute."

"Yes," she admitted, covering his hand with hers, feeling the strength there, needing the compassion. "It hurts."

After all this time, it still hurt.

"I think of him," she confessed, drawing her knees to her chest. "I think of Michael more and more often lately."

She looked over her shoulder, met her father's troubled eyes and shrugged self-consciously at her admission.

"Sometimes...sometimes, I'll see someone in a

crowd and the likeness to Michael will startle me so that for a moment, I actually think it's him.''

Returning her gaze to the fire, she wrapped her arms around her legs and rested her chin on her knees.

"Those damn crank calls haven't helped," her father muttered angrily.

She thought of the phone calls she'd received the past two weeks—the ones where there had been nothing but silence on the other end. The ones that had shaken her enough that she'd stopped by to talk to her brother Drew. When she'd met up with Kristina, Drew's new bride, instead, she'd pocketed the phone numbers of private detectives Tom Reynolds and Lucas Starwind that Kristina had given her.

"I wish you would have called Tom or Lucas, or even the police," Grant added.

She'd been spooked enough by the calls that she'd actually considered calling them—considered, but not followed through.

"They have their hands full investigating the problems you've been dealing with since last December."

Grant grew silent.

The problems all appeared to be tied to the unsolved murders of her grandfather, King Thomas Rosemere of Altaria, her uncle, Prince Marc, and the subsequent attempted assassination of her brother, Daniel, who, as the eldest son of Emma Rosemere Connelly, had taken Thomas's place as king.

Absolutely, the Chicago P.D. and her father's hired investigators had their hands full.

"Besides," she said, "what would I have told them? That I'd received some strange phone calls? 'No. No heavy breathing. No, the calls hadn't seemed ominous.

No, they hadn't felt like pranks, either. Hadn't felt like wrong numbers.'

"It's not much for anyone to go on, Dad, and it wasn't enough for me to follow through with the detectives. And yet..."

"And yet what?" he asked when she paused.

"Last week," she said, speaking more to herself than to her father, "I was walking out of a shop and...it was like I felt Michael there, watching me, waiting for me."

"It's all this business with your grandfather's death and Daniel's attempted murder," her father said with gentle concern. "All the extra security I've had set up is making you nervous. This whole damn situation is making you nervous."

"No. No," she assured him. "It's not that. I've never felt threatened on that front even though I know you've been concerned for me. For all of us. It's... I don't know. Like today in the park. There was a man." Her heart stuttered now as it had when she'd seen him. "I couldn't stop thinking about Michael."

She rubbed her arms, closed her eyes. "Sometimes lately, it feels like he's...still here, Dad."

Her father sighed. "It's because you never had closure."

No. There had never been closure. Instead, there'd been a train derailment in the jungles of Ecuador, endless nights of not knowing, the empty ache of waiting. The helplessness of uncertainty. Of needing to hear. Of wanting to know, yet not wanting to know the worst of it. Then just wanting to know anything.

The jungle was dense and wild, the cavernous cliffs below the derailment site impassable. Michael's body hadn't been the only one that had never been recovered. And Tara had never recovered from the guilt of knowing that the last words she'd spoken to him had been the last words he'd expected to hear.

She still remembered every moment of that day as if it were yesterday. She drifted back to that day at the airport—that horrible day. She could still see the shock and pain on Michael's face in her mind. Still heard the hurtful words....

"You don't have to see me off at the gate," Michael said as he closed the trunk, hefted his flight bag over his shoulder and set his Pullman on the curb by the car.

Around them horns honked, hotel shuttles jockeyed for parking. Travelers hunched their shoulders against the cold, struggled with their luggage, rushed to make their flights.

It was so cold. Cold outside. Cold inside. The bite of it stung her cheeks as she stood there, the collar of her red wool coat turned up against the wind, the air as heavy as the lead-gray sky. Stray snowflakes taunted, promising the bitter Chicago winter to come.

Michael's eyes were troubled as he watched her face. He knew something was wrong. Finally, he knew. After months of combative silences and fractured truths, he finally understood. Finally. Too late.

"We'll talk," he promised as he gripped her shoulders and turned her to face him. "You know I have to go on this trip. It could make or break my promotion, babe." He rocked her gently, lifted one corner of his mouth in that crooked smile she'd never been able to resist.

When she didn't react, he bent his knees, met her at eye level. "When I get back, we will talk."

"It's too late, Michael. It's too late to talk." Her words sounded as frigid as the wind that whipped off Lake Michigan and picked up speed and force as it funneled through the city and cut its way to O'Hare. "It's been too late for a long time now."

He straightened, his hands tightening on her shoulders. He drew her toward him protectively when a woman sprinting for the terminal doors bumped against them with a mumbled apology. His breath puffed out in smoky white clouds of frost that crystallized on the brittle air.

"It didn't feel like it was too late last night."

Last night when they'd made love.

Against all odds, when they could no longer communicate on a verbal level, they'd never lost their ability to communicate in bed.

As she stood there, feeling the heat of his strong hands through her winter coat, seeing the passion in his eyes, she knew that sex had been the only thing keeping them together for some time now.

"Michael...this is hard." She worked up her courage to say the words but she couldn't look at him. "I...I want a divorce."

She felt his shock like the blow that it was. For a moment he was utterly still. Then his hands loosened their hold on her shoulders, dropped to his side.

"You don't mean that," he said after a moment in which they both felt the truth and the finality of her decision like the cut of the wind against their faces.

"Look at me," he demanded, each word a command, each breath an effort. "I deserve to have you look at me when you tell me you want to rip my life apart."

"*Our* life." She raised her head, felt her heart beating with anger and hurt and utter helplessness. "It's *our* life that's being ripped apart, and I'm not the only one responsible. This didn't start here, Michael. Not today."

She felt the tears and couldn't blink them back. "I—I can't do it anymore. I don't want to."

"I don't accept that." His words were as clipped as the wind.

She lifted her chin, looked past him at the glut of humanity crowding toward the terminal doors.

"I'm sorry. But your acceptance doesn't change things. I want a divorce," she repeated, meeting the bleakness and the anger in his gray eyes one last time. Then she turned away.

Like an automaton, she walked around the front of the car, opened the door and slid behind the wheel. She wasn't aware that she'd fastened the seat belt, turned the key and slipped the car in gear. But as she checked the rearview mirror, she was very aware of him standing there. The wind tugged and whipped his dark hair around his beautiful face; his strong cheeks were red from the cold, his gray eyes were set with defiance and denial.

It wasn't until after she'd parked in front of their apartment that she'd realized she was still crying, that she couldn't stop crying.

Tara blinked herself away from a moment that even now, two years later, remained as vivid as Lake Michigan in the swell of a storm. She looked toward the floor-to-ceiling windows of her parents' manor house and felt like crying now.

She still missed what she and Michael had once had. The passion, the hopes, the dreams, the defiance that had them eloping on prom night simply because they were in love. They were in love, but he was the boy from the wrong side of the tracks and she was the princess her wealthy parents wanted to exile to an exclusive girls school to get her away from him. Away from Mi-

chael, who hadn't been good enough for her, who could
never provide for her by Connelly standards.

"John won't wait forever, Tara."

Her father's voice broke through the years, through
the tears she hadn't been able to shed for some time
now. The accuracy of his statement undercut all the
might-have-beens and should-have-beens, and relayed
the truth.

"I know." She laid a gentle hand on Brandon's bottom, needing to feel his sturdy little bulk, to touch what
was real when the surreal threatened to outdistance it.

The door to the den opened with a subtle creak.

"Mr. Connelly, I'm sorry to intrude."

Ruby, dressed in her starched black uniform even at
this late hour, stood in the doorway. Her hands clenched
the doorknob so hard her knuckles had turned white.
Her eyes were as round as the buttons on her blouse,
her cheeks as gray as her apron.

Her father realized that something was wrong at the
same moment Tara did. The unflappable Ruby, who had
been their head housekeeper, a fixture and a friend for
all of Tara's memories, was far from the composed
manager of Lake Shore Manor.

"Ruby?" Grant's brows knit together with concern.
"What is it?"

"Mr. Connelly," Ruby repeated, clearly struggling
for control. "There…there's a gentleman here. He
wishes to…he wishes to see Miss Tara."

"At this hour?" Grant snorted. "And does this *gentleman*—who has the audacity to come to my home
at—" he raised his arm, shoved back the cuff of his
custom tailored white shirt and checked his watch
"—just after nine o'clock in the evening—have a
name?"

A preemptive anticipation had Tara's heart suddenly pounding. Her breath inexplicably clogged in her throat as she rose jerkily to her feet.

If possible, Ruby turned a whiter shade of pale. Her gaze shot to Tara, apologetic, even a little alarmed, and yet guardedly hopeful as she opened the great oak door wider.

A man stepped into the room, a shadow in the doorway, a ghost from the past.

"Good Lord," Tara heard her father murmur in shock and incredulity as Michael Paige's lean, athletic frame filled the doorway.

Tara shook her head, disbelieving, yet wanting, with everything that was in her, to believe. She touched her fingers to her lips, tears brimming as the man's somber gray gaze sought and found hers.

"Michael."

Her father rose to his feet behind her; his strong hands gripped her shoulders, steadying her. But all she could see, all she could feel was Michael.

Blood roared through her ears. Her heart pounded like thunder—in her chest, in her throat. Her legs grew wobbly and weak. Tears stung in a hot, burning flooding of emotions.

Through the watery mist she stared as her husband stood there, his eyes—those flinty gray eyes—warm on hers, unblinking on hers.

He took a step forward and caught her hands in his. She cried out at the shockingly familiar feel of his fingers grasping hers. His grip was hard, his hands callused. Warm. Real. Alive.

She stared down at their clasped hands, aware that hers were shaking, and she studied the strength and the scars—some she recognized, some she did not.

"Tara."

She raised her head at the gruff need in his voice, watched his eyes as he searched her face, then cast an unspoken plea at her father. Her father squeezed her shoulders protectively, hesitated, then with reluctance, dropped his hands.

With his gaze fast on hers, Michael pulled her into his embrace.

She fell into his arms on a sob, clung to him desperately, wept without shame—for him, for herself, for everything they'd lost.

He was here. My God, he was alive. Strong, warm and real. He smelled—oh, he smelled like Michael. She buried her face in his neck, needing more assurance that it was him—really him—and not some horrible trick of imagination and misery and guilt.

His hands roamed her back with a tender urgency, a familiar intimacy that said he, too, was struggling with the reality. His heart beat wild and strong against her breast as he whispered her name against her hair.

She pulled back so she could see his face, to cement into fact that it was really Michael.

The man she had loved.

The man she had asked the courts to declare legally dead.

The man she planned to divorce.

Two

Michael buried his face in Tara's hair, wallowed in the silk and honey scent of her. It seemed like forever since he'd felt the sweet press of her breasts against his chest, her slim hips aligned with his. It seemed like a thousand forevers—and yet it felt like yesterday and the hundreds of yesterdays they'd shared.

He'd seen everything from shock to joy, disbelief to denial, hope to love in her eyes before she'd flown into his arms. He didn't care that her reaction had been knee-jerk, maybe even involuntary. The only thing he cared about was that he was finally holding her.

"Michael...son."

He heard Grant say his name a second time before he reluctantly lifted his head, searched Tara's eyes. He touched his thumb to the aristocratic arch of her cheekbone, smiled gently, then transferred his attention to her father.

The man looked shaken. He appeared to be in as much shock as Tara and Ruby.

Son. Grant had never called him son during the five years he'd been married to Tara. Michael strongly suspected he never would—not when he had steady legs under him. The word had slipped out, a figure of speech, an indicator of just how much his appearance had unnerved the great Grant Connelly.

"Hello, sir."

"Michael, how— What…" Grant trailed off, held up a hand, a gesture of utter confusion from a man used to being in total control.

"I know." Michael read the questions in Grant's eyes. "I know. You have questions."

He looked down at Tara, at her violet eyes, misty now with that edgy mix of disbelief and shock.

"You all have questions."

He couldn't stop looking at her. He wanted to look into her eyes forever. He wanted to take her somewhere. Make love to her. Tell her all the things he'd been dying to tell her since he recovered his memory two weeks ago. But there was more, much more that he'd missed.

Linking his hand with Tara's, needing to touch her, to be touched by her, he looked down at the little boy asleep on the floor.

His child.

He swallowed back emotions so consuming and complex he couldn't put a name to them, blinked back the burn of tears that blindsided him. He did not want to give in to them. Not here. Not in front of Grant Connelly.

"May I?" His words came out gruff and thick with the knot of emotion that clogged his throat.

A long hesitation, then Tara's voice, barely a whisper. "Yes. Yes, of course."

From the corner of his vision, he saw her touch a hand to her mouth, saw a tear leak down her cheek as her father wrapped a protective arm around her shoulders.

He bent down, picked up the stout little bundle and straightened, laying him against his chest. The child snuffled, a sighing, baby sound of contentment, then snuggled against him in his sleep, fearless of this stranger who was his father.

Soft. He was so soft and so sturdy and so vulnerable. He smelled of powder and little-boy smells. The silk of his hair caught in the stubble of Michael's beard; the heat of his hearty little body warmed Michael in ways he'd never thought possible.

"I'd heard that having a child could change a person," he murmured, unaware that he'd spoken aloud.

Something had definitely changed inside him the day he'd seen his son's picture in that tabloid. Changed him enough that it had shocked his memory back. He'd discovered then and there that there was nothing he wanted more than to reclaim his life.

"I'm sorry," he murmured, fighting with his emotions, offering an apology. "I wasn't prepared for this."

The burst of love was so profound he felt the pulse of it thrum through his body in tandem with his heartbeat. He struggled to collect himself, but lost the battle and turned his back on the room. He pressed his face to the sweetness of Brandon's neck, giving in to a sense of longing and loss so absolute that he couldn't stop the tears.

When Emma Connelly hurriedly entered the room on a surprised intake of breath, he was hardly aware that she'd joined them. He was only remotely aware of Ruby—crusty and sometimes crotchety Ruby—dabbing a tissue to her eyes.

"Michael."

Tara's voice was gentle, her hand on his shoulder supportive and full of compassion. It brought him back, reminded him of other obligations.

"Would you…would you like to take him upstairs and put him to bed?"

She understood. He needed some time. He needed some space to compose himself.

He squeezed his eyes tight and nodded. Without a word, he turned and followed her out of the room.

Grant regarded him with granite-hard eyes as he passed him by. Emma touched his arm, squeezed gently. Ruby grinned like a goose and finally made him smile.

He was back. He was home. And nothing—not Grant Connelly, not a legal divorce action and not a man by the name of John Parker—was going to keep him from claiming his wife and becoming a father to his child.

A half hour later Michael was back in the family room. If not completely composed, he was at least determined to field Grant Connelly's questions.

He stood in front of the fire, felt the heat of it through his pant leg along with the burn of expensive liquor in his belly. He'd braced one hand on the mantel, wrapped the other around the snifter of cognac Ruby had thrust at him with a "drink it, you're gonna need it" arch of her brow.

She'd been right. All eyes were on him. The adrenaline rush that had gotten him this far had ebbed, but the liquor had steadied him.

"I'm sorry. I know this is a shock showing up this

way.'' He met Grant's hard gaze, then Emma's. She smiled in encouragement.

''I ran through a hundred scenarios. Tried to figure out a way to make this play out easier for you. Finally, I decided the only thing to do was come over here tonight.

''This has to be very hard.'' He glanced from face to face. ''For all of you.''

''This isn't hard, Michael.'' Emma Connelly sat on the sofa beside Tara, holding her daughter's hand in her lap. ''Losing you was hard.''

Sincerity shone in her kind blue eyes. It made him smile. Grant Connelly's wife loved her husband very much. So much that thirty-five years ago she'd turned her back on the small European country of Altaria, abdicated her rights as princess and moved across the Atlantic to Chicago to marry a man her family regarded as a crass, American upstart. The press still played on the fairy-tale elements of the story—and on the creation of Grant Connelly's dynasty of wealth and power, as well as the lives of his many and colorful children. The Connelly dynasty not only made money for its own, it continued to provide a lucrative source of revenue for the paparazzi.

In addition to loving Grant, Emma Connelly also loved her children—all of them. Tara was no exception. Emma hadn't always been in Michael's corner.

Once she'd understood that Michael loved Tara, however, Emma had done what she could to soften Grant's anger and resentment. She did what she could now. Even though Grant's back was to the room, Michael felt the subtle waves of his anger. He'd expected no less.

With his feet braced for battle, Grant stared through

the French doors that lead to the east terrace. Finally, dramatically, he turned to face Michael.

"I went to Ecuador, Michael. Many of us went— Daniel, Justin, Rafe, Seth—anyone who could manage it. We searched for days. Days, Michael, and came home convinced that no one could have survived that derailment."

"I seriously doubt that anyone did." Michael lifted his gaze from his cognac to Grant's steel-gray eyes that demanded an explanation. Then he dropped his first bomb. "But I wasn't on that train."

He scanned the faces in the room during the long moment it took for them to digest that shocking piece of information.

"What do you mean you weren't on the train? That's why you went down there," Grant insisted when he found his voice. "You were going to inspect... What was it?" He waved a hand through the air, searching his memory. "A new source of exotic wood. Something about a potential supply for Essential Designs."

"That's right." Michael nodded. "The company had sent me down for that reason. I'd flown the first leg to Dallas then on to Quito. And I was booked for passage on that train."

Michael looked at Tara. Upstairs, in Brandon's bedroom, she'd hung back even after he'd pulled himself together. He'd wanted to wrap her in his arms again, kiss her until they were both breathless, make love to her until they were both senseless.

While he wanted all of those things, after their initial embrace, she'd withdrawn into silence. Even now, she watched him with a suspended sort of wonder and a wariness that would have angered him if he hadn't understood what a shock this was for her.

Obviously she needed time to deal with her feelings for him. It was enough to deal with the fact that he was alive. He didn't figure she was ready for the whole story of his disappearance, either, so he cushioned it as best as he could.

"I had an overnight layover in Quito. I had time to kill so I decided to see a little of the city." He stared at his cognac, then at Tara. "Turned out it wasn't such a good time to be out on my own. Essentially what happened was that I got mugged."

When Tara closed her eyes, he was glad he left out the part about being so angry and hurt over their parting words at O'Hare that he'd gotten blind, stinking drunk. He hadn't been sight-seeing. He'd been wallowing in self-pity, nursing his hurt from one dive to the other, effectively making himself easy pickings for the gutter rats that had attacked him.

"Oh, my dear child." Emma's eyes glimmered with tears. "You were hurt. Hurt terribly, weren't you?"

"There's no easy way to say this." He looked away, then back. "They worked me over pretty good. Stole everything I had on me, including my ID. As close as I can piece it together, they must have driven me out of the city, dumped me in the jungle and left me for dead."

Even Grant winced at the last statement.

"But you didn't die."

"No." He met Grant's eyes, gave him the benefit of the doubt that he saw more shock than disappointment. "I didn't die."

He tossed back the rest of his drink, let out a long breath.

"I know this is hard to swallow. The rest is even harder. Long story short, a man by the name of Vincente Santiago found me on the other side of the mountain range. He and his wife, Maria, nursed me back to health. Maria is a healer.''

Michael read the speculation on the faces in the room and knew that his voice had warmed as he talked of the two people who had not only saved his life, but had taken him in as one of their own. There would be time enough later to explain his special relationship with the Santiagos.

"You've been recovering all this time?"

Grant again. Michael thought grimly that he'd have made a good D.A.

"No. It was… I don't know…maybe six months before I recovered physically from the injuries."

"Six months? That was eighteen months ago. Why the hell didn't you come back when you were well?" Grant had moved past stunned and was edging well into anger.

"Why didn't you at least contact us? Tara was half out of her mind with grief. You had to know we were all worried!"

"Grant, if I could have contacted you, I would have. But the problem was I didn't know." He met each pair of eyes, lingered, at last, on Tara's. "I didn't know you were worried. I didn't know anything. I took some pretty good shots to the head in the beating."

He touched his fingers to the scar on his temple, unconscious of the gesture.

"When I finally came around, I didn't know up from down. I didn't know how I'd gotten there, didn't know where I'd come from. Didn't know my own name."

"Amnesia," Ruby muttered. "Lord above."

She marched with single-minded intent to the bar,

uncorked a bottle and helped herself to a shot of her employer's very old and very pricey brandy.

"Yeah, amnesia," Michael echoed. "And you thought it only happened in the movies." Hell, *he'd* thought it only happened in the movies.

"Two years. Two years, Michael? You expect us to believe you just wandered around down there for two years not knowing who you were?"

"Grant," Emma admonished gently. "The boy has been through a harrowing ordeal. For goodness sake. Let him finish."

Michael smiled a thank-you to Emma then addressed Grant.

"As I said, I was a good six months recovering, and learning Spanish," he added with a tight smile. "The Santiagos spoke very little English at that time. The fact that I did was my only link to my identity. I figured I was American, but it didn't narrow things down much.

"And I didn't wander," he added as Grant's frown deepened. "The Santiagos took me in. I worked for them. And then I worked with them, as a partner in their lumber business." There was much more to that story but Michael figured it could wait for another time.

"When…when did you remember?" Tara asked, her brows pinched together. She'd pulled her hands away from Emma's and locked them tightly together in her lap.

"Two weeks ago."

"Two weeks?" Grant's tone and expression made it clear he was still at odds with the story. "What? You just suddenly woke up one morning and remembered you had another life?"

"Look, Mr. Connelly, I know this is hard to accept. Hell, I still have trouble sorting it all out."

"Just take your time, dear."

Michael smiled at Emma again, grateful for her support.

"What did prompt the return of your memory?" Tara asked.

"You," he said without hesitation.

Her face drained to pale.

"You did," he repeated. "You have to know that like the Kennedys or the Trumps, the Connellys are American royalty to the rest of the world. What you do, where you go makes the news—even the international news.

"I was in a Quito equivalent of a supermarket." He paused, rocked, as he was always rocked when he thought of that day. "I was checking out and spotted this trashy tabloid.

"Your face—" He stopped again, drew a bracing breath. "Your face and Brandon's were splattered all over the front page, along with the announcement of your engagement to John Parker. My picture was there, too—complete with the gory details of my death."

"My God." Emma rose shakily and joined Ruby by the sideboard. Ruby poured her a glass of brandy, refilled her own. "How horrible for you."

"Horrible? Yes and no. I've got to tell you, it scared the hell out of me at first. The rush of memories it triggered was staggering. Everything just came slamming back—I apologize for the expression—like a train wreck." Along with an excruciating pain in his head.

"I passed out cold. Must have been quite a sight," he added with a slight lift of the corner of his mouth. "When I came to, I was laid out flat in the aisle along with the contents of three sacks of groceries, and I started to remember. Everything."

He looked pointedly at Tara, knew by the expression on her face that she was thinking about their last conversation. If possible, her face grew even paler.

"I suspect that right now you're all feeling something close to what I felt that day," he continued. "It…it felt like I'd been hit by a two-by-four."

He touched his fingers to his temple again. A sharp, intermittent pain that had become his recurrent friend stabbed through his head.

"Michael!" Tara shot to her feet, raced to his side and touched his arm. "Are you all right?"

"I'm fine." He shook it off, made himself focus, smile for her. "Just a little reminder of the past two years."

"A long two years," Grant put in. He looked from Tara to Michael, appeared to be not altogether pleased that she'd rushed to his side. "I can't tell you how sincerely glad we all are that you're alive."

"But," Michael said, offering the opportunity for the other shoe to fall.

Emma looked pained and apologetic.

"But it's been two years, Michael. Two years," Grant restated for emphasis. "We've heard nothing. Nothing." He paused dramatically for emphasis. "Life has gone on. Tara has moved on."

Michael watched Tara while her father spoke. Despite what Grant maintained, Michael could see that she hadn't moved anywhere. Not yet. And if he had anything to say about it, the only direction she was going to move was toward him.

He was back. And he was prepared to fight. For his wife. For his son. For his marriage. It wasn't a battle he was prepared to start tonight, though, not with Grant Connelly present.

"With due respect, sir," he began as he met the older man's eyes. "I don't think that's a decision Tara's made yet. And when she does, that decision will be between her and me."

It was the deepest part of the night, the hour reserved for lovers. Moonlight danced across tall walls cloaked in ivory damask. Fine linen sheets tangled and slid to the foot of the bed in the second-floor bedroom of Lake Shore Manor where Tara Connelly Paige slept.

The sheer ecru silk of her gown twisted around her hips; a delicate sheen of perspiration misted her throat and her brow. The slender fingers of her right hand clutched a cool spindle of the brass headboard as she moaned in frustration, ached for release.

Her left hand lingered at her breast in an unconscious caress. She dreamed of her lover's mouth there, suckling, adoring. She dreamed of Michael, his gray eyes smoky with desire, his broad shoulders blocking the moonlight, his strong arms caging her in as he braced himself above her.

She sighed his name, arched her back and rode with the wild and stunning pleasure that he gave and took and demanded. His lean hips pumped into hers, his body filled hers as he enticed her to go with him to that place where sensation ruled and passion promised to make her whole again, make her real again, as she hadn't been real since he'd left her.

"Michael," she whimpered and, in her sleep, ran her hand over her ribs, across her abdomen, down to the place that ached for him, throbbed for him. "Michael…"

She sat up straight in bed, wrenched out of sleep by

her own cries. Her breath slogged out in serrated gasps.
She looked wildly around the room.

It was not the apartment she had shared with Michael.

It was her room in Lake Shore Manor.

Where she'd slept. Alone. For two long years.

A dream.

It had only been a dream.

She collapsed to her back on the bed, threw an arm
over her forehead and willed her heart to settle, her
breath to steady. And then she lay there in the dark of
night, in a silence disrupted only by her ragged breaths.
Aching for him. Burning for him.

Michael wasn't a dream. He was alive. She'd seen
him tonight, talked to him, touched him. And right now
she wanted him so badly she hurt.

She missed lying with him in his bed. Missed the
length of him, the strength of him, the heat of his
mouth, the stroke of his hands.

She didn't have to miss him anymore.

Staring hopelessly at the ceiling, she trembled with
the need to call him, to ask him to come to her. To
make love to her.

The ache intensified to pain.

It would be so easy.

And so wrong.

The tears came then. Tears of relief that he lived.
Tears of grief that she hadn't let herself shed since the
day, two years ago, when the news had arrived with its
ghastly presumption of death. Tears for all they'd had,
for all they'd lost.

Michael was alive and she was so glad. And yet the
one thing he wanted couldn't happen.

He'd made it clear. He was determined to pick up
where they'd left off. She dragged her hands through

her hair, drawing on her resolve. That couldn't happen. She could not resume her life with him. She couldn't go through the pain of loving him again. Loving Michael hurt too much. Loving Michael had always hurt too much.

She closed her eyes, rolled to her side and hugged her arms to her breasts. And then she hid in the night and clung to the one absolute that overshadowed his miraculous reappearance.

On this point she could not waiver. For reasons that only she could understand, she was going through with the divorce. She had to. She had to because she knew what no one else did: She was a fake. A fraud.

The image the media and even her family held of Tara Connelly as a headstrong, independent, gutsy and self-assured woman was a lie. A complete sham.

The real Tara Connelly was a wimp. She wasn't strong enough to do much more than drift through life with her emotions tightly under wraps. She wasn't equipped to do much more than heed her survival instincts that warned her to stay under the radar, to exist with as little involvement as possible. Which meant she wasn't capable of surviving another attempt at loving Michael Paige.

And as she lay in the dark, fighting the want, denying the need, she was ashamed of the knowledge that the real Tara Connelly was too afraid to even try.

Three

The next morning Michael started his day waiting for Tara's brother Brett at an affluent Lake Shore Drive condominium complex. He stood in the visitor's parking lot at the address Brett had given him, leaning against the fender of a rented BMW.

Belmont Harbor spread out before him like a watercolor of sun, surf and sails. Pricey pleasure crafts rocked in their moorings; silver-white sails dotted the relatively calm waters of the bay. He felt a million miles away from the lush jungles of Ecuador, even farther from the projects in the rough part of the city where he'd grown up, although the distance in miles was under ten.

"And how many miles do you have to go to get your wife back?" he asked under his breath and thought about everything that had happened last night.

Tara had changed. He didn't think he was wrong about that. Seeing him out of the blue when he was supposed to be dead had been a hell of a shock for her. But there was something…something else that he'd sensed. He hadn't been able to put his finger on it. But he would. He knew Tara. Knew her better than anyone, including John Parker, could ever know her.

A car door slammed behind him. He turned to see Brett Connelly walking toward him, a smile of disbelief and welcome spreading across his face. Michael grasped the hand Brett extended then felt himself pulled into a back-pounding embrace.

"I'll be damned." Brett stood back, gave Michael an assessing once-over with smiling blue eyes. "It really is you. Son of a gun, I thought I'd seen the last of your ugly face. I can't tell you how glad I am that I was wrong."

Michael had always liked the Connellys' youngest son. Both Brett and his twin brother, Drew, were outgoing and friendly. Brett had also had enough of the rebel in him to appreciate Michael's wild streak.

"Well, just goes to show," Michael said, grinning, "nothing's ever over till it's over."

As he'd been leaving the Connellys' last night, Emma had asked him where he was staying. He'd sensed that she'd been on the verge of inviting him to move out of his hotel and into Lake Shore Manor when Grant had thrown her a murderous glare.

"Call Brett in the morning," Emma had said instead, deferring to her husband's unspoken command. Then she'd written Brett's phone number on a slip of paper and pressed it into his hand with an affectionate squeeze.

"Brett's a married man now," she'd said, beaming brightly. "And a new daddy. He and his wife, Elena, just moved into their new house. The last I knew they hadn't yet sold or sublet their condo. It should accommodate you nicely until you're more settled.''

Speaking of settled, it looked like life had done well by Brett. He looked good, really good, as he grinned at Michael part in disbelief, part in pleasure.

"If Mom hadn't filled me in with a 6:00 a.m. phone call, I'd have flat-out keeled over when you called.''

"It's a shock, I know.''

"The best kind. Come on.'' With a hand on his shoulder, Brett steered Michael toward the front entrance of the building. "Let me show you the condo. If you like it, it's yours.''

"I appreciate this, Brett.''

"That's what family's for—and you've always been family, even though it may not have seemed that way at times.''

Inexplicably touched by Brett's warmth, Michael acknowledged his overture with a grin. "Okay, brother, fill me in on this new family of yours.''

Brett did, with a huge smile and a beaming pride that told Michael how happy he was.

"Now fill me in on John Parker,'' Michael said after congratulating Brett on his good fortune. He knew nothing about Parker but what he'd read in the tabloids that had linked him to Tara. Sensationalized news stories were no substitute for Brett's take on the situation.

"What am I up against here?'' Michael asked.

"That's one thing I always admired about you, Paige.'' Brett sobered as he punched in a security code to access the elevator. "You cut right to the chase. Good to see some things never change.

"Parker's a nice enough guy,'' Brett continued after a thoughtful pause. The elevator doors slid open.

"He's quite a bit older than Tara. She doesn't love

him,'' he added with a contemplative scowl as they entered the elevator. The car rose in hushed precision to the top floor. ''I take it you've seen her.''

''Last night.''

Michael had to force the words as he digested Brett's news. Tara didn't love Parker. The relief nearly sent him to his knees. He hadn't realized until that very moment how much the possibility had been eating at him. It would have made a difference if she'd loved Parker. Michael would like to think he'd have been able to be a man and walk away, knowing she was happy.

He drew a bracing breath and followed Brett with a lighter step to the far end of a long hall and what Michael had decided were the penthouse suites.

Brett slipped a key in the lock and shoved open the door. They walked through the airy foyer and into a spacious living room. A bank of floor-to-ceiling windows surrounded the room on three sides.

Brett strode across the room and with the push of a button, opened the vertical blinds. The view of Lake Michigan from twelve stories up was breathtaking.

''Nice,'' Michael said, taking in the dining area at the far end of the living room and the kitchen just beyond it.

''Bedrooms are this way.'' Brett nodded toward the hall then headed in that direction. ''Two, and two baths. Oh, and the basement garage has assigned spaces.''

''How is she?'' Michael asked without preamble.

Brett met Michael's eyes without blinking, seemed to consider how much he should reveal, then just let it go.

''She's not Tara the Terror anymore. After you 'died' the old Tara disappeared.

''It's not good,'' Brett added grimly. ''She's too quiet, too... I don't know. It seems like she's just drifting. Oh, she loves Brandon and protects him like a mama bear but she's lost all of her spunk, you know? Hell, I can't even get a good rise out of her anymore and you know how she likes to argue.''

Brett shook his head, like he was trying to pin things down himself.

''I think…well, my gut instinct tells me that she agreed to marry John—you've probably already figured out that Parker's one of Dad's associates—because he can provide stability for Brandon.''

Michael clenched his jaw.

''It damn near killed her to lose you,'' Brett continued, his eyes on Michael. ''Brandon seems to be the only thing she really lives for. She just plays at her job at *City Beat.*''

''*City Beat?*''

''One of Chicago's latest and greatest forays into the publishing industry.'' They walked down the hall, Brett talking as he opened bedroom doors, showed Michael the closets.

''It's one of those trendy, upscale magazines—fashion, interior design, city living, that sort of thing. Tara's a consulting editor for the interior design segments. Part-time,'' he added. ''I don't think she's particularly passionate about it. It's more like it fills the time for her.''

''Interior design, huh?'' Michael poked his head into the guest bedroom.

Tara had studied interior design at the University of Chicago. He was glad she was able to do something with her degree. He'd insisted that she go to college even though it was all he could do to pay the rent and put food on the table during those early days of their marriage.

"Lots of rooms to fill here," he said then met Brett's thoughtful gaze. They exchanged a conspiratorial look. "Looks pretty bare."

"What you need is a good interior decorator," Brett said with a grin.

"Yeah. That's exactly what I was thinking."

"Look," Brett said, suddenly sober, "I know things were a little rocky for you and Tara before Ecuador. I don't know what happened between you two and I don't want to know. That's your business. But she's my sister and I love her. You want her back? Then you see to it that you make her happy. All right?"

"I want her back. And I want her happy."

"That's good enough for me. Anything I can do to help?"

"Nope, but thanks for the offer. This is something I need to handle on my own."

And it was something he intended to handle—as soon as he figured out how to convince his wife that what was right between them five years ago was something he could make right again.

Michael made the fifteen-minute drive from the condo to Lake Shore Manor in record time. He was still having a little trouble readjusting to the Chicago race pace. Time stood still in parts of Ecuador. Many times during the past two years he'd very much enjoyed being a part of those time warps. Since returning to Chicago, he'd actually found he missed them. He'd missed Tara more.

After the gatekeeper buzzed him in, he pulled up in the circular drive, climbed out of the BMW and stared at the classic Georgian mansion that was located in the city's most fashionable neighborhood. A calm settled over him along with a comfortable realization. He wasn't the same man Tara had wanted to divorce two years ago. That man had been hungry for power, determined to succeed, both intimidated and angered by this palace and all it represented.

No, he wasn't the same man. And Tara, evidently, wasn't the same woman. She was still the woman he'd fallen in love with, though. She was still the woman he wanted.

After another long, thoughtful look at Connelly Manor, he started up the steps, suddenly missing his grandmother, missing his mom who had struggled to make ends meet and been rewarded for her hard work by death at the hands of a drunk driver. Michael had been ten.

Shaking off the melancholy, he pressed the bell, then returned Ruby's wide smile when she opened the door and showed him inside.

"I'm past my shock now," she confided as she drew him into a laughing embrace. "Lord above but it's good to see you, you handsome devil. I hope you're here to bring that girl back to her senses, and back to life for that matter. She hasn't been our Tara since you left us."

Michael had always liked Ruby. She was sometimes gruff, but she always told it like it was. And she didn't mind interfering in the business of the family she'd served for nearly thirty-five years.

"If it doesn't work out, I don't suppose you'd consider running off with me. You know I've always had a thing for you, Ruby."

"Go on with you." She swatted his arm. "Always were a smooth talker. You come on in now. She's expecting you."

When he'd left the manor last night, he'd asked if he

could return the next day to talk to Tara and to see Brandon. They'd agreed on 9:00 a.m. It was 8:50.

The calm he'd felt earlier suddenly deserted him. He chalked it up to fatigue. He'd lain awake staring at the ceiling in his hotel room until well past two reliving the first full day of his resurrection.

Resurrection. What a word. And how fitting. After his memory had returned, he'd felt suspended in a half world of what was and what had been. The old Michael Paige was not fully alive yet. Even after he'd made the decision and had returned to Chicago, he'd felt suspended somewhere between yesterday and tomorrow, here and now, as he'd debated how best to approach Tara, agonized over what her reaction would be. But now the worst was over, the best was yet to be and he truly did feel reborn.

Oh, it wasn't all over, he conceded as he smoothed a hand down his tie. He hadn't won her back. But at least he wasn't lurking in the shadows anymore, searching for a glimpse of her, longing for a look at his son.

His lips twitched in self-derision as the term stalker came to mind. He could smile about it now but for those first few days back in the city, that was exactly what he'd felt like. A stalker following his own wife, calling her on the phone and then chickening out at the last moment when she'd answered.

It was not among his finer moments. No. He wasn't proud of either his actions or his mind-set during that first week back in the city. But he gave himself a little latitude on that count. He was still recovering from the shock of learning about his other life. His life before Ecuador.

The small, recurrent stab of pain he'd been experiencing since recovering his memory shot through his temple. He felt it less frequently now; the bite was not nearly as strong. Dr. Diamanto had told him it would lessen and eventually abate all together. Yet he felt it now as he thought of the Santiagos.

They'd wanted to come to Chicago with him. Both Vincente and Maria had wanted to be with him when he encountered the disbelieving stares, the stunned astonishment, the look on Tara's face when she saw him.

"It will not be an easy thing for you, Miguel," Vincente had said carefully as they'd discussed details of the business operation that needed attention in Michael's absence. "Nor will it be easy for her."

He had smiled at this man who had taken him into his home without question, at the woman whose healing hands and sweet compassion had seen him through the most difficult period of his life. And he'd been reminded, as he hadn't been reminded in the years since he'd lost his mother and then his grandmother who had raised him after his mother died, of the unqualified love and importance of family. The Santiagos were his family now.

Tara and Brandon—they were also his family. Never more than now did he realize how important it was to win her back.

"As much as I appreciate the offer, this is something I have to do myself," he'd told Vincente. He hadn't wanted to hurt him or Maria but he'd needed to see this through on his own. As always they had understood.

"And as much as we would like to help, we respect your decision," Vincente had replied. "Go with God, my son."

All of these thoughts flashed through his mind as he followed Ruby through the foyer as tiny rainbows of color, reflected from the hundreds of dripping Waterford crystal prisms that hung from the massive chandelier, danced across the gleaming white tile floor.

"She's not alone, I'm sorry to say," Ruby groused over her shoulder as she showed him down the spacious and richly appointed central hallway toward the sunroom.

"You know Grant. Protect and provide. Emma's with her, too, so she'll soften the way some."

"Sounds like I could use someone in my corner."

"My money's on you, Michael. Always has been. You're a street brawler and a hard head and you never did know when to quit. I'm betting you won't be quitting now." She squeezed his arm and left him.

No. He wouldn't be quitting now. Squaring his shoulders, he gathered himself, then simply stood for a moment and looked at the only woman he had ever loved. And he knew, without a doubt, that what he said in the next hour might make the difference between winning her back or losing her again—this time forever.

September sunlight, as crisp and crystalline as the morning, sparkled through the floor-to-ceiling windows of the sunroom. Tara sat in a fan-backed white wicker chair, oblivious to it all. Her coffee cooled, untouched on the table beside her. She stared without seeing at the fall flowers blooming in a riot of dazzling color on the patio just outside the French doors and the maze beyond. And she waited.

Before he'd left last night, Michael had asked if he could see her again. He wanted to talk to her. He needed to see Brandon. When she hadn't been capable of anything more than a carefully controlled, "Of course," he'd told her he'd be back in the morning. Nine o'clock.

She glanced at the Cartier watch John had given her on her twenty-fifth birthday in May and felt a pang of guilt. On its heels, a ripple of excitement, made sharper by anxiety, sent her heartbeat racing.

It was 8:55 a.m. Michael wouldn't be late today. He'd never been late—until his career had become more important than she had ever been. Then everything had changed. He'd been late too many times to count during their last year together.

She wet her lips, counted to ten, willed her heart to settle. And still it pounded. She couldn't wait to see him again, yet dreaded seeing him. Then Ruby was there, showing him into the room and the waiting was over.

She turned her head slowly. He stood in the doorway, tall and strong and alive. How many times had she yearned to see him that way again? How many times had she heard a voice, seen a face that made her think of him and long for him and know she could never have him?

The sight of him took her breath away, made her already stuttering heart go haywire. He'd always done that to her. From the first moment she'd set eyes on him he'd sent her senses reeling. She'd been fifteen. She'd also been a spoiled little prima donna, insisting on attending public school so she could experience the real world.

Michael Paige had been as real as it got. The day she'd seen him strut across the lunchroom with his laughing gray eyes, his thick, jet-black hair and his looking-for-trouble grin, she'd known he was exactly the kind of trouble her parents had tried to protect her from her entire life. She'd wanted him at first sight. She still did.

That was why this was going to be so hard.

"Michael." Emma rose from the chair beside her at his gruffly murmured, "Good morning."

Tara watched her mother clasp Michael's hands in hers then kiss him softly on the cheek.

"I still can't believe it." Both wonder and warmth filled her mother's voice.

Her father rose as well but his welcome was as cool as the fingers Tara clasped together on her lap. He extended his hand.

"Michael," Grant said with a grim nod.

Michael returned her father's handshake then shifted his attention to her. His gray eyes bored into hers, then roamed her face as if he were memorizing her features. Then he smiled—that wonderful heart-melting, knee-weakening smile she remembered—and she had to look away to keep from returning it.

She didn't want to return his smile. She just wanted to assure herself that he was okay, really okay, and then she wanted to get on with her safe, pristine, façade of a life. Without him.

"With all of the…let's say, stress last night, I don't think I told you how wonderful you look, Mrs. Connelly," Michael said.

Tara noticed, as she had last night, that his voice was deeper, his carriage, if possible, even more proud. No. Pride may not be the correct word. As she watched him, she wasn't sure what it was that she saw.

He'd changed. Last night, even as shocked as she'd been, she'd sensed the changes his experience in the jungles of Ecuador had made in him. Michael had always been strong. It seemed he was even stronger now. He'd always led with his chin and with a bold arrogance that had turned his life into a competition. He always had to have the best, be the best, beat the best.

She could feel this new strength in the way he dealt with her father. The bold arrogance was absent, though. A new confidence, both understated and steady, had taken its place.

He'd changed in other ways, too. There was something dark and mysterious, like the boy she'd fallen in love with, yet…different.

He was still the same man, however, she reminded herself, the man who had been so driven by his goal of success that he'd shut her out of his life and not even realized that he'd left her behind.

"Well," her mother said when the silence in the sunroom lengthened to the point of discomfort. She walked with purpose to her father's side, linked her arm through his. "We'll just leave you two. I'm sure you have many things to talk about."

"Emma." At her mother's unexpected intervention, her father's face grew as dark as a thunderstorm. Clearly Grant Connelly hadn't planned on going anywhere.

"Come along, dear," Emma insisted, a steel in her voice Tara rarely heard when her mother addressed her father. "We'll be in the library if you need us, sweetheart."

And that was the end of that. Her father shot a warning glare at Michael before he left the room, but he left, and that in itself, was a minor miracle.

Now she was alone with her husband. Her husband who had been dead for two years. There was so much she needed to say to him. Unfortunately, there was very little that he would want to hear.

Michael sent Emma a look of gratitude as she dragged Grant out of the room. He wasn't exactly sure why Emma Connelly had chosen to park herself firmly in his corner but he wasn't going to question it. He needed all the help he could get.

He turned to Tara. She was ghost pale, her hands clenched in her lap, her eyes too wide, too bright and too determined to avoid his.

Fragile. She looked fragile and vulnerable, not at all like the sassy hellion who had set her sites on him ten years ago, damn the torpedoes—and the consequences.

Maybe it would help to remind her that they had both been different people then, that life was about growth and changes that could strengthen, not diminish their love.

"I remember the first time I saw this place," he said carefully.

Instead of sitting beside her and dragging her into his arms like he ached to do, he made himself walk to the French doors and stare out over the complex and meticulously kept maze.

"I was fifteen and this monument to your daddy's fortune intimidated the hell out of me." Just like Grant Connelly had intimidated him, Michael thought grimly.

"I've got to tell you, it was a hell of a culture shock for a fifteen-year-old outlaw who had never known his own father. Outlaw being the operative word," he added with a rueful grin.

Back then, he'd had to use whatever means available to help put food on the table. Some of them legal, some of them stretching the limits.

He turned back to her, searched her face. Nothing. No change in expression. Nothing to say. She hadn't asked him to leave yet, so he took it as an invitation to stay, and to continue.

"I had a chip on my shoulder the size of the Sears

Tower." With a tight smile, he shoved his hands deep into his pockets.

He'd worn a chip, all right, along with the angry pride of a boy who'd been raised by the streets and by the stern but loving hand of his grandmother. It still amazed him that she'd never given up on him. But then again, maybe it wasn't all that amazing. He didn't intend to give up on Tara, either.

"Since my memory returned," he said, bringing himself back to the present, "it's been like... How do I explain it? Like a running newsreel. Little pieces of my past shoot by or stop on freeze-frame while I focus on them, put things in perspective.

"One thing I've found out, Tara," he said, still very aware of her silence. "Your father doesn't intimidate me anymore."

"I noticed," she said and for the first time, he saw a hint of a smile.

Encouraged by that small sign, he continued. "I still can't buy and sell Connelly Corporation. I wanted to once, though," he added and returned her smile.

"And now you don't?" she asked doubtfully.

"Now I understand how much my blind ambition added to your unhappiness." His insatiable need to best her father had driven a wedge between them that had pushed her to ask for a divorce.

"I didn't see it, Tara." He raised a hand in conciliation. "I swear to God I didn't realize how miserable I'd made you—and for that, I'll always be sorry."

"I believe that you're sorry," she said evenly. "But it doesn't change who you are, Michael."

He frowned. "You used to love who I am."

She looked down at her tightly clasped hands.

"Tara, what do I need to do to convince you that

I've changed? That this experience has changed me? That money is no longer my primary focus? That even though I still can't best your father, I honestly no longer feel the need to?''

He could have told her then that he could shop in the same stores as Grant Connelly now, dine in the same restaurants, rub elbows at the same clubs. That he had money now. The fact was, he was rich—thanks to the Santiagos and the staggering growth of the business he'd helped them build during the past two years.

He could have told her, but he held back. He didn't want her believing him because money had erased his motive. He wanted her believing him because she understood that it wasn't the money that had changed him. And it wasn't the money that mattered now. It was Tara. It was getting her back.

''Remember the first time we quit dancing around each other with long looks and flirty smiles and actually talked to each other?'' he asked, abruptly changing tack, taking them both back to a time when all that mattered was how much they loved each other.

Violet eyes met his with hesitation and a stubborn attempt to remain distant, untouched and silent.

''Freshman study hall, second week of school,'' he said, filling in the silence and painting a picture he knew she carried with her, just as he did.

''We'd been working up to it for over a week.''

She looked away and he pressed on.

''You were the princess. I was the pauper. You were a good girl with a yen to go bad and I knew exactly what you saw when you looked at me. I was your ticket for a walk on the wild side.''

That statement earned him her full attention.

''I fell in love with you then, Tara. Knowing that you

were so far out of my league that I couldn't even afford the cheap seats, I still fell in love with you. I'm still in love with you.''

She closed her eyes, looked past him to the window. "Michael…I'm so sorry for what you've been through. And I'm so very glad that you're alive.''

His heart thumped him hard, and refused to level. "But?''

"But love wasn't enough then." She wet her lips, still wouldn't look at him. "It's not enough now. I'm sorry, but I'm going through with the divorce.''

Four

Michael clenched his jaw, shoved his hands deeper into his pockets and tried to make her think about what she was saying.

She loved him. Him. And he refused to believe she would follow through with the divorce. Just like he refused to believe that her relationship with Parker could ever compare to what they'd had, what they could still have.

"Love wasn't enough," he said, throwing her words back in her face, "but what you have with Parker *is?*"

She rose, her motions stiff and unnatural as she walked to the window, touched her fingers to the glass.

"What I have with John is what I need."

"And what is that? What *exactly* is it that you have with him?"

He could see her reflection in the glass, could read the emotion she tried unsuccessfully to guard from him.

"Security. Respect. Stability."

"You could get that from a bank," he said, and watched her shoulders stiffen.

"I don't...I don't wish to discuss my relationship with John."

"Do you love him?" He had to hear it from her.

"I...I care for John."

"Do you *love* him?" he repeated.

She closed her eyes and had nothing to say about that.

"You don't. Because you still love me," he insisted.

When she didn't deny it, he moved to stand behind her. He was so close he could smell the floral and meadow fragrance of her hair. So close he could see the thrum of her pulse fluttering beneath her jaw.

If he raised his hand, he could touch her cheek, curve his fingers in a caress along the slim line of her throat. He ached to touch her there. To be asked to touch her there.

When she didn't ask, he did it anyway.

"There's a flower in the rain forest." A slight tremble eddied through her as he skimmed the back of his fingers over her jawline. "Don't ask me the name. I don't know. But it fascinated me. The petals are unbelievably soft, a shimmering, nearly liquid translucence. The color is incredible—ivory flowing to peach. You make me think of it. It makes me think of you."

"Michael, don't."

"You're trembling." His voice was gruff and low as he turned her to face him.

He cupped her shoulders in his hands and forced her to look at him. Watching her eyes, he trailed his index finger along the pulse point just above her collarbone.

"Your heart is racing."

He ran his hand along her arm, laced his fingers with hers. "So is mine."

Lifting their clasped hands to his chest, he pressed her palm against his heart. "Feel what you do to me. Tara—"

"Don't," she interrupted miserably. Her eyes, alive with sexual heat, searched his before she broke away, frantic to put a foot then two more between them.

"You want me to tell you I didn't miss you? That I didn't miss what we had in bed? Well, I did. Every moment. Every day. Every night. I still do."

Her confession would have heartened him if every word hadn't been heavily laced with shame and anger over what she obviously considered a weakness.

And yet, she missed him. That was what he chose to hang on to.

"We don't have to miss each other any longer."

"Sex wasn't the answer to our problems." She held up a hand, stopping him cold when he would have moved closer. "It still isn't."

"It was never just sex between us."

"You're right. It was more. It was anger and resentment and disillusion."

"Tara—"

"No. Let me say this. We were young. We both fell in love with ideas and ideals and images of what we thought we were. *Who* we thought we were."

"I've always known who you were."

"And I've always known that I was never what you needed."

"You were *always* what I needed," he insisted, moving toward her again. "Always. You still are."

"No, Michael. What you needed was to *be* someone.

It's what you lived for, to the exclusion of all else. In the end I felt the most excluded of all."

"I know." He shoved a hand through his hair, felt the deadly accuracy of her accusation like a gut punch. "I know that now."

"*What* do you know? What *exactly* do you know? Do you know that I'd lost you long before you disappeared in Ecuador? Do you know that I tried everything I could think of to make you understand how much I missed being an important part of your life? How much I wanted you back?"

Blind ambition. That was what he'd been about back then. That was what had brought her to this. What had brought them to this.

"Tara, I didn't realize what was happening to us."

"So you said. But now you know. Now that you've come back from the dead."

There was fire now. In her eyes. In the heat of her slim, sleek body as she moved with agitated grace.

"That's great, Michael. That's wonderful. But how long will it be before the rush of returning wears down? How long before you'll gear up again, retool, refocus and set your mind to the next conquest?"

"Tara, you have to believe me when I tell you I'm not the same man you were ready to divorce two years ago."

She smiled sadly. "I'm not the woman you left behind, either."

He regarded her for a long, searching moment and for the first time admitted that he was not at all sure of what he was seeing. "And do you like this new woman?"

A strangled laugh burst out. The soft sound bounced

off the glass walls of the room like the ghost of the woman she had once been.

"Like her? *Like* her, Michael? I don't even know who she is." She crossed her arms over her midriff, cupped her elbows in her palms. "I'm not sure I ever did. The only thing I know for certain is that I can't survive you again."

"Survive me? Tara, for God's sake, this isn't an endurance test."

"Isn't it? Wasn't it?"

He narrowed his eyes, felt the involuntary flex of the muscle in his jaw. "It'll be different this time. I'll be different. Except for one thing. I love you. That won't change. And you love me, not Parker."

"I think there's an old Tina Turner song that sums it up nicely." Again, that sad, cynical smile. "What's love got to do with it?"

She met his eyes squarely for the first time. "What's love ever had to do with it?"

Michael knew in that moment how much of a fight he was going to have to wage if he was going to get her back.

Brett was right. She wasn't the same woman. This woman had decided there was no such thing as happily ever after, nothing but foolishness in the notion of a forever kind of love. This woman had conditioned herself to resist feeling or reacting or relying on her heart to call the shots for her. This woman no longer believed in the man she'd wanted him to be.

Her fight is gone, except when it comes to Brandon, Brett had said. Brandon she would love and protect with everything that was in her. The next words out of her mouth confirmed it and gave Michael back a small measure of relief.

"I won't keep you from Brandon." She looked at him then. "He needs his daddy."

"And I need his mother." The words burst out, unedited, unqualified. No pride. He had no pride left.

And she had no intention of acknowledging it. Eyes distant, voice steady, she told him how it would be.

"Again, I'm sorry, Michael. I…I am so glad you're alive. So very, very glad. But I can't be your wife anymore."

"But you'll be Parker's," he ground out. Anger and frustration, fueled by a total and complete loss as to how to reach her, made him reckless. He made no attempt to hide his contempt.

This time when she looked away, he wasn't having any of it. And he wasn't having any more of this cold, dispassionate woman he didn't know and wasn't sure he liked. He wanted Tara back. The old Tara. And right or wrong, he was going to take a wild stab at finding her.

He snagged her arm, pulled her flush against him. Desire shot through his blood, hot, potent, demanding. And when he felt the sizzle of it arc between them, he knew she wasn't as resistant as she would have them both believe.

"Can he give you this?" Too full of anger, too far gone on need to do anything but take what he'd been missing for two long years, he lowered his head and covered her mouth with his.

Instant heat, spontaneous arousal. He dragged it all in through the touch of his hands on her body, through the warmth of her mouth against his. The taste of her, the feel of her against him—he grasped it like a last breath, like a first breath, like a life-giving breath that was both hers and his and was essential to sustaining them both.

She surrendered against him on a sound that was part protest, pure hunger and absolute need. This he remembered. The melting heat, the instant yearning. The essence of her had been a part of him even when he hadn't known who he was or that she was the woman he longed for.

"Tara." Breathless, he lifted his head, met violet eyes glazed with desire, and dove back for more. He took more until her mouth wasn't enough for either of them.

On a ragged breath, he dragged her harder against him. With his hands in her hair, he tipped her head back and lost himself in the misty longing in her eyes.

"Take me somewhere. Anywhere. I need to be alone with you."

Her expression was dazed, her breath came in short, shallow pants as she searched his eyes until the sound of footsteps behind him brought her back to her senses. She darted a glance over his shoulder, paled and braced her hands on his chest as if to push him away. He held her fast.

"Tara?"

Michael stiffened at the unfamiliar voice that was infused with propriety.

He watched her face as her eyes chilled.

"John." It was more breath than word, more embarrassment than acknowledgment.

This time when she pushed shakily out of his arms Michael let her go. He turned slowly, sized up the man

in one long, assessing look. Early fifties, polished, mon-
eyed. Cold as a fish.

He turned back to Tara. *This is what you want?* his
eyes asked. *He's what you want?*

"Everything all right in here?"

Michael worked his jaw, watched his wife, then
turned and extended his hand.

"I don't believe we've met. Michael Paige," he said
coldly, "Tara's husband."

"John Parker." Parker ignored both Michael's hand
and his statement. "And that would be my fiancée
you're mauling."

"Interesting choice of words." Michael managed a
tight smile. "Considering she's still my wife."

"Don't." Tara moved to stand between them.
"Please. Don't do this."

"It's all right, darling." Parker regarded Tara with a
reassuring smile. "I have no intention of causing a
scene that would distress you. I'm sure Mr. Paige agrees
that there's every reason to be civil."

"Mr. Paige," Michael said pointedly, "was having
a very civil word with Mrs. Paige until you interrupted."

Parker expelled a long-suffering sigh. "Your father
was concerned about you, my dear."

Because she was upset, and because he didn't want
to turn this into a pissing contest with the head skunk,
Michael chose to ignore the slight.

He turned back to Tara, folded her cold, cold hands
in his.

"This isn't over. *We're* not over," he said softly,

then placed a long, soft kiss on her brow. "I'm going to see Brandon, okay?"

Before she could react, he turned, wrapped a companionable arm over Parker's shoulders and steered him smoothly and forcefully toward the door.

"Ever been to Ecuador, Parker?" he asked conversationally. "Amazing country. Very advanced in many ways, startlingly primitive in others. For instance, let me tell you a little story about how the natives in the Ecuadorian jungles deal with poachers..."

"Have they sent up those page proofs yet, Chloe?" Tara asked absently as she reached into her desk drawer, grabbed a Hi-Liter and marked a section of text she planned to edit.

"I think so. Just a sec. I'll check."

Tara didn't look up from her desk as her assistant, Chloe Chandler, just out of college, full of vitality and confidence, flew out of her office. It took all of her concentration just to keep her mind on the work in front of her after Michael's unsettling visit to Lake Shore Manor this morning.

"Here they are." Chloe breezed back into the office with a beaming smile in her voice. Her blue eyes sparkled as she shoved a fall of honey-gold hair behind her ear and set the pages in front of Tara.

"And they look great. You're gonna love how the bedroom shots turned out."

"Thanks."

"Not a problem." Chloe turned to leave Tara's office then stopped short with a breathless, "Whoa. Sorry...I didn't hear you come in. Can I, um, help you?"

"I believe I've found what I'm looking for, thanks."

Tara froze. She didn't have to look up to know what, or in this case, who, had Chloe so rattled. She'd recognize that voice anywhere. Any time. In her sleep. In her daydreams. And now, it seemed, in her office.

She looked up into Michael's smiling eyes then glanced quickly at the normally articulate and never speechless Chloe, who seemed to have gone into a trance. She appeared rooted to the floor. Her face was flushed, one hand fluttered at her throat. Her eyes were all for Michael.

"Hi." He was all smiles, oblivious to Chloe's reaction. "This a bad time?"

A bad time? She had a feeling she was always going to have a bad time when Michael made an appearance.

"No. No, not really." She made a great show of aligning a stack of material with the hope of appearing unaffected.

"Great. Thought maybe I could take you to lunch."

She blinked. "Lunch?"

"Yeah, lunch. You know, that little meal between breakfast and dinner?" He winked at Chloe and she nearly melted into the carpet.

"Even—" He paused, looked back at the title plate on her door. "Even consulting editors need to break for lunch, right? Aren't I right, Ms....I'm sorry. I didn't catch your name."

"Um," Chloe turned a brilliant shade of red then got a hold of herself. "Chloe. Chloe Chandler. I was...I was just leaving."

Chloe scooted to the door, then turned back to Tara.

Making sure Michael couldn't see her, she fanned herself and mouthed, "He is sooo hot!"

While the scowl she shot Chloe told her she didn't appreciate her reaction, Tara understood it. Even though she told herself she wouldn't think about such things, she remembered having the same reaction the first time she'd seen Michael. The fact that she had felt her own cheeks flush and could think of absolutely nothing to say didn't mean he still had that affect on her. She just...well, she hadn't recovered from this morning. From seeing him. From his determination. From his kiss.

His kiss.

Oh, how she'd missed his kiss. And his strong, lean body pressed against hers.

Snapping her thoughts back to the here and the now, she cut herself a little slack. Yes, he rattled her. Again. But she hadn't expected to see him so soon. And certainly not here, where she worked.

Every time she saw him it was a shock—and not just because he was alive after she had finally reconciled herself to the idea of his death. It was the jolt of her heart that danced at the sight of him. Of her breath quickening. Her palms growing damp.

He was dressed in soft, faded jeans and an oatmeal-colored V-neck sweater. He'd shoved the sweater's sleeves up forearms that were tanned and strong and dusted with fine, dark hair. The same dark hair peeked from the V-neck of his sweater. A vivid image of her fingers playing through that chest hair, then drifting lower, to his taut belly where that silky hair narrowed and arrowed—

Enough. She made herself concentrate on this moment, schooled her gaze to his face.

"I thought you were spending the rest of the day with Brandon." After their meeting in the sunroom earlier this morning, he'd asked and she'd agreed that Michael should spend some time with the boy.

"I am." He angled a thumb over his shoulder. "One of the receptionists—Marcie, I think—snagged him the minute I walked in the door and wouldn't give him back. Quite a charmer, our son."

Our son. She drew in a bracing breath and tried not to let herself be affected by the sound of it, the feel of it, or even by the fit of it.

"How have you two been getting along?" she asked, because it seemed like a safer topic than lunch and because she had been concerned. Brandon was a healthy, happy little boy, but he was sometimes shy around strangers. Sad fact that it was, Michael was a stranger to him.

"Great." He crossed his arms over his chest and leaned a broad shoulder against the doorframe. "You've done a good job with him, Tara."

She looked down at her hands, saw she had them clasped too tightly together. She snagged a pencil from a black leather holder sitting on the corner of her desk in the hope it would make her appear less tense. Then she ruined the effect when she bobbled it and in her haste to catch it, sent it sailing off the edge of her desk.

"Hey. Relax, okay?" he said softly. He pushed away from the door and walked across the room to retrieve the errant pencil.

"I'm not here to pressure. Honest," he added when

she arched a brow in doubt. "I just wanted to see you again. And I wanted to apologize for this morning. I'm sorry I came on so strong. It's just a little overwhelming for me yet.

"Sometimes this rush of…I don't know, I guess you could call it want, just gets a hold of me and, well…" He held up a hand. "Anyway, I'm sorry. I didn't mean to frighten you."

"You didn't frighten me, Michael."

She would go to hell for lying. He'd scared her to death. He still scared her. She was too susceptible to him. To his looks. To his touch. To everything about him that she couldn't let herself give in to. Not if she wanted to salvage some of herself.

"Good," he said, smiling again. "Because the last thing I want to do is scare you, or make you nervous or uncomfortable around me. So, that's why I'm here. To try it again.

"So here's the deal. I wanted to see you. And I knew Brandon would want to see you, and I knew you'd want to see him so I figured, hey, three out of three ain't bad. And here we are."

She had to smile at that logic.

"So what do you say? Can you join us for lunch?"

It was tempting but then, Michael had always been a temptation. For that reason, and for all the temptations he would throw in her path, she had to resist.

"I don't think I can manage it today. My schedule's really full."

"No, it's not," Chloe said, popping her head back in the room. She glanced from Tara to Michael and back to Tara again.

"Sorry. Didn't mean to eavesdrop." She gave a sheepish shrug. "I was just passing by the door, and, um, overheard. The art department had to postpone the meeting until tomorrow so you're clear for the rest of the morning. As a matter of fact, you're clear for the rest of the day," she put in cheerfully, then sobered when she caught Tara's stone-cold glare.

Chloe had picked a fine time to find her voice again.

"Well, I'll just…I must have some filing to do," Chloe said weakly.

Michael grinned as Chloe's head disappeared behind the door.

"Looks like you're free as a bird. Just lunch, Tara," he added, sobering. "I promise. No pressure."

Just lunch. If only it were that simple. But nothing in her life was going to be simple anymore. She'd just as well get used to it.

"I'll get my jacket." Resigned to learn here and now how to deal with the complications Michael would bring to her life, she pushed away from her desk and walked to the coatrack.

Michael, in the meantime, had decided that he liked Chloe on the spot, as well as Marcie and the rest of the women who had swarmed around Brandon then cast sly, speculative looks his way. The word, evidently, had gotten out. Not-so-subtle whispers had followed him down the hall after he'd been directed to Tara's office.

"That's him."

"Him who?"

"Michael Paige. Her husband."

"Michael Paige? But I thought he was dead!"

"Oh, honey, if that gorgeous hunk is dead, then this is the Great Beyond and we've all gone to heaven."

Not only did they relish the juicy fact of his appearance, they seemed to approve of it because he got a couple of covert thumbs-up as he balanced Brandon on his hip and held the door open for Tara as they left the office.

He grinned goodbye to the women huddled around the reception desk, all making a bad show of looking busy and fighting against craning their necks in the hopes of catching any last comment as the three of them walked out the door.

Unreasonably buoyed by their obvious approval, Michael felt better and better about the tack he'd decided to take. It had become apparent this morning when he'd met with Tara that he wasn't going to win her back with pressure. From the stiff set of her shoulders and her closed look when Parker had interrupted them, she was getting enough pressure from him. Her father, no doubt, had been applying the screws, too. Emma, however, had proven again that she supported not Grant, but him in this.

"Don't you worry about Grant." Emma had pulled him aside after his meeting with Tara in the sunroom. "I can handle him. As a matter of fact, he's already coming around, albeit grudgingly."

"He wants what's best for her," Michael had conceded.

"Well, that's not John Parker. John is a dear and Grant may have once thought he was perfect for her, but I've always known he wasn't for Tara."

"You didn't always think that I was, either," Michael had said with open speculation. "What changed your mind?"

She'd regarded him with warmth and affection as they started up the wide, curving staircase that led to the bedroom suites and Brandon's room.

"The day we lost you was the day we lost Tara. I knew then that we had never given you enough credit for making her happy. I want our old Tara back, Michael. So does Grant. We miss that fiery little hell-raiser who used to laugh and cry and live her life like she was riding the front car of a roller coaster."

"There's something to be said for merry-go-rounds over thrill rides," he offered fairly.

She shook her head, smiled. "Not for Tara. Not for you."

He was silent as they walked the carpeted hall to Brandon's playroom, then paused outside the door.

"Did you know she'd asked me for a divorce just before I left for Ecuador?"

Emma nodded then grasped his hands, squeezed gently. "No marriage is perfect, Michael. Lord knows, Grant and I have had our problems."

It was the first time he'd ever heard Emma allude to the period of time in their past when Grant had strayed. While Grant's short affair with his former secretary, Angie Donahue, wasn't a subject that was often broached, Tara had confided in him about it, explaining that the end result was her half brother, Seth.

That disclosure had helped define the special relationship Tara and Seth had always shared. The two of them had always been rebellious and despite the eight years that separated them, they'd always been close because of it.

Seth hadn't become a part of the Connelly family until he was twelve years old when his mother had finally decided she wasn't cut out to be a single parent or capable of managing the handful Seth had become. Grant had sent him immediately to military school to clean up his act. So yeah, he'd been rebellious, just like his new little sister, Tara, who was too young to prejudge him as a punk when almost everyone else had.

"I'm counting on you, Michael," Emma had said warmly. "I'm counting on you to fix the problems in your marriage.

"Can I offer a little advice?" she had asked gently.

"I'm open to anything." Even he had heard the desperation in his voice.

Emma had smiled. "Don't try to coerce her. She's troubled right now and confused. And she's under enough pressure as it is. Take the low road, Michael. Try to remind her, with subtle ways and gentle persuasion, why it was good between you once and why it could be good between you again."

The memory of Emma's words brought him back to the moment and the woman by his side and the child in his arms. Emma was counting on him.

Now, as he and Tara and Brandon descended from the twenty-fifth floor that housed *City Beat's* suite of offices, he told himself he was counting on someone, too. He was counting on Tara to listen to her heart and eventually realize they were meant to be together.

If that kiss they'd shared this morning had been any

indication, she was already weakening even though she didn't want to.

Emma's advice was sound. Two years ago he wouldn't have had the patience for a slow and subtle courtship. He had it now. He also had something else. Something John Parker didn't have. He had a history with his wife—more good than bad—and the determination to win back the most important element of his life.

"Where are we going?" Tara asked after they'd buckled Brandon in his car seat.

"On a picnic," he said brightly as he checked the rearview mirror. "You'd like that, right, buddy?"

He caught Brandon's bright eyes in the rearview mirror, and was once again stunned as he looked into his gray eyes. He was a miracle, their son.

"Michael, it's barely sixty degrees out today and the wind must be gusting up to twenty or thirty miles an hour."

"Not to worry." His smile was secretive and smug. "I've got it covered."

He had it all covered. Feeling more at peace than he had in a very long time, he pulled out into traffic and set about the business of getting his life back.

Five

Twenty minutes later they swung into the Lake Shore Drive condominium complex. Tara frowned.

"This is Brett's old building."

"Mine now," Michael said as he pulled into the underground garage. "I'm subletting his unit."

That made her nervous, he could tell, so he tried to dispel the wariness in her eyes.

"It worked out great for both of us. Brett hadn't had a buyer yet and while room service does have its advantages, I don't particularly like living in a hotel. I want to move in here as soon as possible. Too much of a nester, I guess."

Nester. Did that word trigger memories for her, too? Beside him, Tara walked toward the elevator in silence as he carried Brandon and a picnic basket Ruby had packed for them. Was she remembering their first apartment?

He'd driven by it a couple of times since he'd returned to Chicago. It never failed to bring vivid and pleasant memories, like the one that drifted into his consciousness now…

They'd been married a week, had been staying with her brother, Seth, until Michael had been able to scrape together enough money for a deposit and the first month's rent on a place of their own. He'd wanted to find a place where she could walk to class so they'd ended up north of Hyde Park and the University of Chicago, which were like an island of affluence amidst this very poor section of town.

Michael had watched her eyes as they stood in the doorway of a dumpy little one-room walk-up on the fourth floor. Chalky gray paint peeled in blotchy flakes from the outside door molding. The hallway smelled disgustingly like someone had used it for their personal restroom. She tried to hide the horror with an overbright smile as he turned the key and swung open the door.

"It's…intimate," she said after a long, tense moment in which her huge eyes had taken in the cracked ceiling, the bare lightbulb hanging from a central fixture, the camper-sized refrigerator and hot plate with a dangerously frayed cord.

"Like…like a little nest," she added, swallowing back her shock and gamely widening her smile.

She was eighteen. She was used to household staff and unlimited lines of credit. She'd probably never made a bed in her life, never so much as boiled water. He'd taken her from luxury to near squalor in five easy steps—and in that moment, he'd never loved her more.

He lifted her into his arms, this violet-eyed beauty who could have had any man she wanted but had chosen him. She had an inner fire and spunk that shined through her eyes, and as young as she was, she was savvy and self-assured. And she was fiercely protective of those she loved. Even now her bright smile protected him from her disappointment and fear over what she'd gotten herself into.

"It's only for a little while," he'd promised as she looped her hands over his shoulders and he carried her over the threshold.

"It doesn't matter. It's ours. Only ours and I love it!"

"You can't love it." He laughed and pressed his forehead to hers. "It's an ugly little hole."

"No," she insisted, "it's a home waiting to happen. It's our home. Our nest."

They made love on the floor that night where they slept huddled together in his sleeping bag. That and a beat-up radio were their sole pieces of furniture.

"I love you, Tara Paige," he murmured as he held himself above her, her face cradled in his hands, her body naked beneath him, lush and damp with the heat of their loving.

"I'll never make you sorry for marrying me."

Eyes closed, she smiled a sleepy, sated smile and slid her legs up and along his, then wrapped them around his waist.

"I love you, Michael. Always. Forever. And there is nothing you could ever do that would make me sorry."

He kissed her then, long and deep, then slid down her body, pressing kisses as he went, loving the slide of her skin in sweet friction against his. Loving the feel of her velvet-tipped nipple against his tongue, her silky sigh of pleasure, her uninhibited cry of surrender as he made love to her with his hands and his mouth and his soul.

The next morning he'd given her the last one hundred dollars he had to his name.

"This needs to stretch until payday, babe. That's gonna be a long five days."

When he came home that night he was stunned by the spicy scent of marinara sauce and garlic wafting from the apartment. He smiled at the fresh coat of deep purple paint that coated both trim and door. When he opened the door with his key, he was dazed all over again.

He stood there and would have wondered if he'd stepped into the wrong apartment if his wife of seven days hadn't been waiting for him inside, her eyes shining with excitement and barely guarded anticipation of his reaction.

He looked from her to the once bare lightbulb that was now covered with a colorful paper shade. A small studio sofa sat in the center of the room, covered with a floral slipcover in soft shades of blue, mauve and gray. Beneath the table, a worn tapestry rug covered the stark and barren gray tile floor. Twin, battered tables of an unidentifiable wood painted deep navy flanked the sofa; dozens of cream colored candles, all sizes and shapes, flickered from every available surface.

He smiled through his worry. She had to have blown the entire hundred bucks and then some.

"It's beautiful," he said, forcing back his concern about their immediate financial situation in the face of her hopeful smile.

"It's home." She threw herself into his arms and offered him a stack of folded bills. "There's still thirty-some dollars left," she said beaming.

He blinked, fisted the money. "How?"

"I called Ruby." She flew out of his arms, touched

a hand lovingly to the sofa cover. "Told her I needed to do some shopping. Oh, Michael, she showed me the most fascinating places! Little flea markets, secondhand stores and bargain basements tucked here and there around the city."

"Tara Connelly at a flea market?" A doubtful but proud grin tipped up both corners of his mouth.

"I'll have you know," she said saucily, "I've discovered a talent for finding bargains and for making deals."

"You," he said, pulling her back into his arms, "have a talent for making me happy. I'm the luckiest guy in the world."

"Better hold that thought until after you've tried my marinara sauce." She looped her arms over his shoulders. "Ruby gave me a crash course on that, too, and I made enough to last the rest of the week so you'd better like it a lot."

"I like *you* a lot." He kissed her, ran his hands down her slender back, cupped her firm, high buttocks in his palms and pulled her snug against him.

"Um, you know, we *do* have a sofa now." She smiled against his mouth as he lowered her to the floor.

"Hmmm," he managed as he whipped her snug T-shirt over her head and went to work on her bra. "And a very nice one, too." He stripped her jeans and panties down her slim legs. "How did you get it up the stairs?"

"Seth and Brett. It, um, makes into a bed."

He lifted his head, eyed her like she was the most brilliant woman on earth. In his eyes she was.

"Luckiest guy in the world," he repeated, "and as soon as I show you how happy you make me, we'll christen that sofa bed good and proper."

"You don't have a proper bone in your body." She sighed as he touched her where she loved for him to touch her.

"And it was the very improper Michael Paige that I fell in love with. Don't— Oh, Michael," she sucked in her breath when he entered her in a long, slow stroke. "Don't change on me now."

The elevator settled with a subtle ping. The doors glided silently open, dragging Michael back to the present. The vivid and erotic memory of them making love, however, lingered.

"Well, here we are," he said, hoping she didn't notice that his hand was a little unsteady as he walked them down the hall and inserted the key in the condo lock.

"It's a step or two up from that little apartment down on Front Street."

His gaze sought hers and held. In that brief moment, he knew that she had been thinking about that first apartment, too. It had been ugly and small and they had constantly fought roaches and miserable plumbing, but they'd had some of the happiest days of their marriage there.

"Welcome to my humble abode." With a sweep of his hand, he invited her to walk in ahead of him.

He set the picnic basket on the counter and Brandon on the floor with a soft pat on his bottom.

"Nice, huh?"

"Nice and empty." She stood hesitantly inside the door, as if she were wary of coming any farther into his condo—or into his life.

"I was thinking maybe you could help with that." With casual ease, he opened the basket and started setting food on the counter.

She turned to him, a protest forming on her lips.

"I'm hoping to have Brandon over here often," he explained, preempting her flat-out rejection of the idea. "I want him to be comfortable. I don't know what he likes, and let's face it, I don't have a clue what makes things safe for him. You could make sure I don't mess up on that count. Not to mention I obviously need a decorator."

Biting her lower lip, she turned to watch Brandon as he toddled around the empty living area like it was his own huge, private playpen.

"I'd pay you, of course," he added just to see what kind of reaction he'd get.

"Pay me?"

"I want the best, Tara. You turned a one-room roach hotel into a palace—and on a shoestring. Imagine what you could do with this place on a no-limit budget."

"No limit?"

He smiled. For all of her wealth, Tara was one of the least materialistic women he'd ever known. He'd also known she would be intrigued by that statement, could see on her face that she was dying to ask when and how money had become a seemingly endless commodity.

She didn't ask and he still didn't want to tell her. In the end, he was hoping she would eventually feel comfortable enough, open enough, to question him about it.

"We've got wine." He held up a bottle, showed her the label, then smiled. "And milk, for my main man here," he added as Brandon came tooling around the corner of the counter and wrapped his arms around Michael's legs with a squealing laugh.

It hit him then as Brandon reached for the sippy cup. The enormity of his return. The precious existence of his son. His son, whom he had not seen born, who had grown into this loving, trusting, laughing child who clung to his leg with one hand and to his plastic Lion King cup with the other. He bent down on one knee, ran a hand over his hair, then folded him into his arms and simply savored him.

"He's so…perfect, Tara," he managed. "So absolutely perfect."

Brandon began to fidget, his hyperactive little body and inquisitive mind already intent on exploring more of the wide open space of the condo.

With a pat on his bottom, Michael let him go. He rose slowly and, without meeting Tara's eyes, fished around in the basket until he found a corkscrew. In silence, he went to work on the foil wrapper around the neck of the wine bottle.

"I don't even know how to explain what it feels like to see him, hold him." He swallowed, shook his head. "Sorry. I didn't intend to get maudlin on you. It just…it just hits me sometimes. What I've missed."

He tugged the cork free, stared at the wall for a moment, then turned to her, his expression grave.

"I told myself I wouldn't ask this." He shook his head, gave it up. "Did you know? Did you know about him when I left?"

He watched as she slowly shrugged out of her coat, then stood with it folded over her arms in front of her like a shield.

"No. I didn't know. I…I think I must have conceived that last night," she said quietly.

He stilled, watched her face until she met his eyes. He saw her memories there. Her pale skin beneath black lace. His rough, needy hands, dragging it off of her.

Her cheeks flushed pink and she looked away, walked to the windows and stared out at the harbor. They'd made love in a fury of goodbyes tempered with anger. He'd known she was angry with him.

He hadn't known she was going to ask him for a divorce.

In retrospect, he realized that there had been desperation in her lovemaking that night. Apparently she'd thought it was going to be their last time.

To this point, it had been—and not just his last time with her. He'd been celibate for two years now.

"You and Parker—are you lovers?" he asked abruptly, surprising them both with his bold question. He hadn't known how close to the surface that question had hovered, or how badly he wanted her answer to be no.

"And please, don't tell me it's none of my business," he added gruffly. "Just level with me. Are you lovers?"

"No," she said after a long moment. "We're not lovers."

He let out a breath, closed his eyes and waited for the world to settle. His hands weren't as steady as he'd have liked as he filled two glasses. He walked across the empty room, handed one to her.

"To the future." He watched with stone-faced relief as she lifted her glass and sipped.

To us, he added to himself, more determined than ever that there would be an "us." That there would be a "them." Again, and better than ever.

To the future.

Tara drank deeply of the wine Michael had poured her and told herself she couldn't think about the future. Not now. Not until she had it sorted out in her mind. For the time being, the past and the present seemed a much safer topic.

"You've been out of touch for a long time, Michael," she said carefully. "There's much that's happened in the family that you should know about."

She'd been debating with herself about this. How much did she tell him about what had transpired in the family in the past nine months? Though she was determined to go ahead with the divorce, by law, they were currently married. Michael was entitled to the courtesy of information, no matter how difficult it was going to be to relay some of it.

And then there was the question of how much she really *did* know about these horrible and disturbing circumstances that had plagued the Connelly family lately. She knew her father and suspected that he was withholding information—from her and from some other siblings—because he thought it was for their protection.

She realized she'd been woolgathering when Michael crossed the room and stopped directly in front of her. He placed a finger lightly between her brows like he used to when he wanted to erase her frown lines and relieve her worries. Once, a kiss would have followed. A kiss that she'd have been glad to melt into.

Because she wanted to melt into him now, she walked away, busying herself with draping her coat over the island in the kitchen.

"I'm sure that a lot's happened, and I'm guessing from the look on your face that not all of it's good." His voice was gentle; his brows were knit with concern. "Tell me."

She decided to start with the basics, with what she knew. He'd find it out eventually from someone anyway and he had a right to hear it from her. Fortified with another sip of wine, she began.

"Last December my grandfather and my uncle Marc—"

"Were killed," he cut her off abruptly. His eyes searched hers even as she sensed he was searching his memory.

"My God. I remember reading about it. And I remember thinking then that those names pulled at me and I didn't have a clue why." His voice matched the edgy shock that spread across his face as he probed his memory further.

"The newspapers in Ecuador—and I imagine all over the world—were filled with the news that King Thomas Rosemere and his son, Prince Marc of Altaria, had died in a…what? A boating accident, right?"

"Oh, Tara." He joined her at the counter, took her hands in his, then folded her against him. "I'm so sorry. Your mother must have been devastated."

Because she wanted so badly to accept what he offered, and because she'd resisted him for what seemed like forever, she gave it up. She let herself lean on him, let her arms wrap, with familiar ease, around his waist. He was warm and solid and strong. And she'd missed him.

Because she would always miss him, she pulled away, wrapped her arms around her own waist and walked back to the window.

"It was hard. It's still hard," she admitted as she stared at the busy harbor twelve stories below. His presence behind her was a reminder that he was there for her if she would just reach for him.

"Harder still when it came to light that their deaths weren't an accident."

"Not an accident? What are you saying?" he asked after a protracted silence.

She drew a fortifying breath, turned back to him. "I'm saying that they were murdered.

"Wait." She held up a hand when he opened his mouth to interrupt her. "They were murdered," she restated gravely. "All the evidence points to it. And that's not all. When Daniel, who, according to Altarian law as my mother's eldest son, became heir to the throne, someone attempted to assassinate him, too."

"Daniel? Good Lord. Is he all right?"

"He's fine," she assured him quickly, then bent to lift Brandon into her arms. Poor little guy. He must have sensed the tension in the room. He'd suddenly stopped his seemingly endless romp around the apartment and come running to her side with his arms raised.

She cuddled him against her, pressed a kiss to the top of his head and pointed out the boats in the harbor to distract him.

"Your brother, Daniel. A king." Michael was clearly in a state of shock over the news.

"Remarkably, he's proving to be a fine one, too. As well as a fine husband. Yeah," she added with a small smile. "Once he met Erin it was all over but the shouting. Justin took Daniel's place as VP of Marketing at Connelly Corporation."

"Justin? I suppose you're going to tell me that he's married, too."

"Not yet, but he and Kimberly are engaged. Alex and Phillip—Phillip is the Prince of Silverdorn—also committed to each other. You can imagine what an elaborate event that will be."

So unlike our wedding, she thought, remembering that cool spring evening they'd driven to Missouri and awakened a justice of the peace who'd groused but finally agreed to marry them.

"You already know about Brett and Elena," she added, steering her thoughts away from a time when everything had seemed simple and honest and real, secure in the blanket of young love.

Don't. Don't go there, Tara. Just don't.

"And then there's Drew," she hurried on. "Just last month he and Kristina tied the knot."

He blinked, then blinked again. "I don't even know what to say anymore."

"Well, you'd better sit down because there's more."

After a long stare, he simply folded his legs under him and hit the floor.

"How do I say this?" She bit her lower lip, then took a deep breath. "I guess I'll just lay it out. We've brought two more Connellys into the fold recently. Like Brett and Drew, they're another set of twins. None of us, including Mom or Dad, knew that Chance and Douglas existed until late last winter.

"An investigative reporter was covering the deaths of my grandfather and uncle and turned them up," she continued when she realized Michael was too stunned to even formulate another question.

"Before Dad met Mom, he'd been involved with a woman. Hannah Barnett. Apparently, they'd broken off their relationship before Hannah realized she was pregnant. For whatever reason, she never told Dad about the twins, just like she'd never told them about him."

She watched his face as this new information settled. "I haven't gotten to know them as well as I want to yet, although I very much like what I know of them so far. Doug's a doctor. He and his wife, Maura, are due to have a baby soon. Chance is a Navy SEAL. He and Jennifer have a little girl, Sarah. She's just a little older than Brandon."

She watched as Michael pinched the bridge of his nose between a thumb and forefinger and let out a huff of a laugh that wasn't really a laugh.

"Incredible." On a deep breath, he met her eyes. "That leaves Seth, Rafe and Maggie, right? Or are they all married, too?"

She smiled, thinking with affection of her other siblings. "Actually, no. I can't imagine anyone getting Seth or Rafe to settle down. Seth, well, I worry about Seth. He's in a bad place right now," she added, hurting for him, then hurrying on and offering no explanation.

"And Rafe—well, he's very satisfied with his bachelor life and last I knew saw no appeal whatsoever in marriage or the compromises that go with it. As for Maggie—she's wrapped up in her art and following her free spirit wherever it leads her. I can't see her building a nest any time soon, either.

"But my cousin Catherine, Uncle Marc's daughter— I think you met her at Christmas one year—is married now to Sheikh Kaj al bin Russard. Their story is like something straight out of the Arabian Nights."

Michael was silent for a long moment, his handsome face becoming increasingly grave. He finally rose, took Brandon from her when he saw that she was having difficulty managing his solid and wiggling weight.

"What you said earlier about your grandfather and your uncle being murdered and about an assassination attempt on Daniel. What's that all about? I can't believe it was the result of something as extreme as an attempt to overthrow the Altarian government."

"No. Nothing like that. In its history there's never been civil unrest in Altaria."

"Then what?"

"It's all under investigation." At a loss to deal with

the unsteady flutter of her heart when he looked at her that way, she walked back to the counter, topped off her glass and at his nod, refilled his. "Dad and the boys are pretty tight-lipped about it."

"Who's investigating?"

"Initially Dad hired someone based in France. Albert Dessage, I believe is his name. Daniel's also got Altaria's royal police on it. The Chicago P.D. got called in, of course. In fact, that's how Brett met Elena. She's with C.P.D. and was assigned to the case.

"This June, however, when Elena withdrew because of her pregnancy, Dad decided to hire Rey-Star Investigations, a private agency here in Chicago, to assist. Tom Reynolds and Lucas Starwind, who founded the company together, have an excellent reputation so we're hoping they'll turn up something soon. It's all been very disheartening."

She watched his face as his quick, insightful mind worked through the information she'd given him.

"Okay, let me get this sorted out. First, if this all happened in Altaria, why is the Chicago P.D. involved? And second, if I remember right, your grandfather died in December. That was nine months ago. I don't get it. Why isn't this thing resolved?

"And third, if his death wasn't an attempt to overthrow the government, that means there's something else at stake. And that could mean that all of the Connellys could be in danger.

"Including," he added with a dark and concerned scowl, "you and Brandon."

Six

Tara shook her head and quickly reassured Michael that he needn't be worried.

"At first, yes, Dad was concerned about that. In fact, he added several security measures around Connelly Corporation headquarters and around Lake Shore Manor. But it's been several months now and nothing more has happened."

"But?" he inquired, hearing the qualifier in her tone.

"But it's become apparent that the situation wasn't just limited to the Altarian monarchy."

She drew a deep breath and exhaled.

"Just recently evidence has been turned up that points to a link—possibly with organized crime here in Chicago. And to answer your first question, that's why CPD was called in."

Michael's scowl turned fierce. "Organized crime? My God, Tara."

"I know. Believe me. We all know."

"There's more, isn't there?"

She had rarely been able to hide anything from him. Today was no exception. She hated this part. Hated it.

"None of us want to believe it but there's evidence suggesting that Uncle Marc may have been involved."

"How exactly?" Disbelief, pure and raw, made his face go slack.

She hesitated, debated again how much of this to get into with him. In the end, she simply decided he was entitled to hear everything she knew.

"It seems that Uncle Marc had hidden a gambling problem for years. He died heavily in debt.

"Shortly after Uncle Marc's death, my cousin Catherine found an e-mail Uncle Marc received from some guy who called himself 'The Duke.' The note was some kind of assurance to Uncle Marc that his debts would be reduced for every week that he made sure no one interfered. Interfered with what, we don't know, but it turns out that this Duke person is known to the authorities as an international go-between who specializes in making introductions between aristocrats and organized crime."

Nodding, absorbing, processing, Michael took it from there. "So, if a certain crime family wanted to see a certain law weakened or ignored and was willing to pay, say, a prince with a gambling problem, the Duke would be their man."

"So it seems," she said, impressed by his reasoning power. "And if all this isn't enough— Seth's mother, Angie Donahue showed up a couple of months ago.

"It's killing him. He's been so quiet since she returned. He won't talk to me. He won't talk to anyone. At least, not about her. It's got to hurt, you know? She's his mother and yet twenty years ago she just delivered him—a twelve-year-old-boy—to Dad and Mom like he was a bag of laundry and then conveniently forgot to pick him up again. Until now. Her reappearance is just a little too much coupled with everything else that's been happening.

"Everything's such a mess," she added, feeling so badly for Seth, confused and still saddened by the loss of her grandfather. Missing Daniel, who was thousands of miles away in Altaria and was the one who could always make her laugh.

"And then in the midst of all this," she pressed on, "Connelly Corporation computer systems crashed a few months ago for no apparent reason. It's up and running again now but it was a pretty dicey situation for a while. Dad's been as tense as an air traffic controller ever since, and Charlotte—you remember Charlotte Masters, Dad's executive assistant?"

He nodded.

"Even Charlotte, always cool, always efficient and always in control, has been walking on eggshells and acting very peculiar for the past several months."

"It sounds like she has good reason. It sounds like everyone has good reason," he said with a quiet resolve that had her meeting his eyes. They were dark, determined and even before he spoke the words, she knew what he was going to say.

"And it still sounds like I have good reason to stay as close to you and to Brandon as I possibly can."

Although she didn't say anything, Michael saw a shadow cross her face, noticed a sudden stiffness straighten her shoulders. She wasn't comfortable with his statement. That was fine. It put them on equal footing because he'd grown increasingly uncomfortable as she'd related the unsettling news about her grandfather and her uncle and Daniel.

"Daniel, a king," he said aloud, still having trouble wrapping his mind around that bit of news.

"Wait a minute," he said suddenly as another thought struck him. "If Daniel is king, that makes you and your brothers and sisters princes and princesses, right?"

"Technically, yes." She shrugged and she dug into the picnic basket. "Although none of us have any intention of laying claim to the titles." She sat down on the floor across from him and got comfortable.

"I hate to break this to you, sunshine, but blood tells. You're a princess, official title or no."

That made her blush. It was very beguiling, that blush. So was the slender column of her throat as she concentrated overhard on setting her glass aside and coaxing Brandon to sit down beside her.

Yes, she was as regal as a princess but she was also as warm and nurturing as an Earth Mother as she ran a hand over Brandon's silky hair and started pumping him up about eating his lunch.

For a while, that was where the conversation settled—on convincing Brandon to drink his milk and eat his chicken so he could have his cookie. The issue with her grandfather and her uncle and Seth's dilemma upset her. Hell, it all upset him, but it was Tara's interests he had in mind.

He didn't want to add to her discomfort by pushing her for more information—information she may not even have. Grant would have it, though, and as soon as he could arrange it, he and his father-in-law were going to have an in-depth conversation. He needed to know what kind of danger Tara may be in. And then he needed to make sure nothing happened to her.

Intentionally, he let the conversation veer further away from organized crime and unsolved murders. Their dialogue drifted over little snippets about her mother's and father's health, the ages of her brothers' children, due dates for upcoming blessed events and wedding dates. Brandon's favorite food, favorite stories, favorite toys.

She, too, picked her ground carefully, he noticed, staying with the safe topic of her family while studiously avoiding asking him any direct questions about the time he'd spent in Ecuador, about what his plans were now that he was back in Chicago. As Brandon fell asleep, his head on her lap, Michael decided to open the proverbial door for her and see if she'd step inside.

"So," he said, gathering the remains of their lunch and tucking it into the basket, "how are you doing with this? With me?" he clarified when she frowned.

"You've had less than twenty-four hours to process the fact that I'm alive, that I'm here. You have to have questions. You're entitled to answers. More answers than I was able to give you last night."

Okay, Tara. Your move, his silence stated. And then he waited. Waited until he was sure she intended to stay her own course and keep her distance by refusing to satisfy what had to be a raging curiosity. Waited while he worked to control his own very insistent and compelling need to close that distance both emotionally and physically.

He wanted his wife. He wanted everything about her. Wanted to feel the sensations he so vividly remembered—his hands on her bare skin, his mouth on her breast, his body clenched deep inside hers.

He ached with want. He tasted it, breathed it. And the only thing that kept him from reaching out and taking what he knew she would give if he pressed her was his son. His son, who slept like an angel, not even aware that their future as a family depended on his daddy's ability to keep his cool, to take it slow, to do everything in his power not to scare away this woman who they both loved more than life.

So he waited. He didn't reach out, didn't draw her near, until finally, she let out a deep breath and took the plunge.

"After you recovered physically, why didn't you try to find out who you were, Michael? Surely the…Santiagos, wasn't it?"

When he nodded, she continued.

"Surely they would have helped you."

Well. He hadn't expected her to start there, but at least she'd started. For many reasons, this was the hardest question for him to answer. He decided to be totally honest.

"I'm not sure myself," he finally admitted. "You'd think it would be a top priority, wouldn't you? A man wakes up with no memories, in a foreign place, among strangers—even kind strangers—you'd think he'd want to know something about himself, about where he came from, who he'd left behind, who he'd been."

"Yes," she agreed. "You would think so."

He set the picnic basket aside then stretched out on his side, facing her. Crossing his legs at his ankles, he propped himself up on an elbow and reached out to touch Brandon—just touch him—with his other.

"Wish I had a good answer for you. The one I have you're probably not going to like."

She looked so sad. "I don't think that what I like really comes into play here."

Oh, but it did, he wanted to tell her. It very much did. Because what she had once liked was him. Him holding her. Loving her. And it had never made her sad.

He'd like to think that what happened next happened because she couldn't help herself instead of because he'd made her nervous when he'd stretched out on the floor within touching distance. Whatever the cause, he liked the effect.

She'd gone perfectly still, except for her eyes. Violet and vibrant, her eyes were busy, busy looking their fill, busy taking him in.

Unconscious of what she was doing, unaware that he was watching her, she started at his feet and traveled slowly past his thighs, lingered, as her face reddened, on the growing ridge beneath the zipper of his slacks, before she appeared to force herself to continue upward.

He became as still as she, the caress of her eyes suddenly as intimate and arresting as the touch of her hand. His skin warmed beneath his shirt, his sex stirred. She blinked and met his eyes—a panicked check to see if he'd noticed. Discovering that he had, she looked away, embarrassed.

The heat her gaze had generated in his body slowly chilled to a sobering reality. She would continue to fight this—her attraction, her desire, her love that he was certain she still had for him—until the end. She'd given him her reason this morning.

"I can't survive you again, Michael. I can't survive loving you."

As if loving him amounted to war.

Struggling with the anger that notion generated, he

sat up and faced the bank of windows and the lake, ever aware of her own struggle to keep from watching him.

Okay, he'd concede that maybe toward the end, it had been a little like war. A cold war. But it hadn't always been that way and he was infuriated enough over her statement that he decided maybe it was time for her to hear it all.

"I think," he said, working to keep his voice level as he returned to the conversation that had dropped them into this hole, "that the reason I didn't try to find out my identity was because somehow I knew I wouldn't like what I turned up."

She said nothing, effectively telling him she might not like the reason, either. He owed it to them both, however, to tell her.

"When my memory finally did come back, it was…I don't know. It was really odd. It returned almost sequentially, starting with the first time we met. The first time we made love."

He glanced at her over his shoulder. She swallowed thickly and refused to meet his gaze. He looked back at the lake. Hitching up his legs, he propped his forearms on his knees and clasped his hands loosely in front of him.

"Only after all the good came back, did I remember the bad—like the last time I saw you at O'Hare when you asked me for a divorce." He studied his hands, tapped his thumbs together as he pondered.

"I think that subconsciously I must have held on to that little bit of memory and didn't want to face it. Didn't want to find out who I was because I didn't want to face losing you."

"Michael," she said. Just Michael. Just his name, but the single word held a sea full of roiling emotion. Most of it was regret; much of it was a stubborn resolve to make him understand that they were over. Truly and completely over.

Well, he had resolve, too, newfound and as serious as a heart attack. To that end, he was going to stay the course. He was not going to pressure her into coming back to him.

Emma was right. If he pressured her now, most likely he'd get an answer he didn't want to hear and then she may never be open to an alternative.

Just as Dr. Diamanto had told him he would do, she, too, would react to the shock she was still feeling over finding him alive. She'd retreat into what felt safe for her. And what felt safe for her right now was denying her feelings so she wouldn't get hurt again.

The Santiagos had taken him to see Dr. D. after he'd passed out in the supermarket then awakened with his memory bombarding him like artillery fire. They'd been concerned about his headaches, which the doctor had assured them all would recede to nothing in time.

"Don't make any life-altering decisions for a while yet, Michael," the doctor had said, very aware that Michael had been struggling with where he went from here. "Don't count on your mind to be up to formulating conclusions or making choices that you may have to live with for a very long time.

"A shock of this nature affects the mind's ability to sort out emotional decisions from logical ones, good decisions from bad. That's not saying that logic always outweighs emotion, especially in matters of the heart," he had added kindly.

Michael had confided in him about Tara. He'd had to talk to someone and he'd practically talked the poor doctor's ears off.

In any event, it only made sense that Dr. Diamanto's advice could apply to Tara, too. While Michael had known from the beginning what he wanted to do, he didn't want Tara making decisions about them right now. She needed more time to deal with the reality after assuming he'd been dead for two years.

In the meantime, she was here with him. Skittish as a mouse in a room full of cats, but she was here. That had to count for something. And because it counted, he was determined to make the most of the time he had today and every other day until she came to the conclusion that their marriage was worth saving.

Or until she convinced him there was nothing to save.

"You'd like the Santiagos," he said, changing course and giving them both a much-needed reprieve from the intensity of their emotions. "You'd love Ecuador. It's almost unbearably beautiful. Especially this time of year."

Leaning back on an elbow again, he told her about it. About the lushness of the mountains, the pristine beaches, the exotic rain forests, bustling cities and quaint, colorful villages. Most of all, he talked about Vincente and Maria Santiago.

"Vincente's land was handed down to him from his father and his father before him. It's rich with exotic lumber, ironically, the same type of lumber I'd been sent to search for by Essential Designs."

At the time of his trip to Ecuador he'd been vice president in charge of sales at Essential Designs—having worked his way up from delivery boy, the position he held after school when he was fifteen.

"Vincente has this amazing natural affinity for wood and he'd been doing well selling to local buyers when I came into the picture. He'd been wanting to expand his market for some time and didn't know how to go about doing it.''

He continued talking while Tara shifted her weight off her left hip and settled Brandon more comfortably on her lap.

"It's odd. I couldn't remember my name, yet I could remember everything I'd ever learned about wood, about textures and luster and durability and, most important, about a European market that was clamoring for specialty woods that grow in abundance on Vincente's land.

"Like I said, he'd already realized that he needed to reach more buyers and had made a shaky foray into advertising on the Web. Again, the knowledge was just there for me. We set up a Web page and had over a thousand legitimate hits during the first two months. It just snowballed from there and it seemed overnight we became a major player in the exotic wood market.''

She'd been gently brushing the baby fine hair back from Brandon's temple, watching him sleep, but now her head came up.

"We?''

He smiled. "I'm a full partner in the business now. It was Vincente and Maria's idea. I fought it at first. I was afraid that I was taking advantage of the fact that they'd never had children and had started looking upon me as a son, just as I had grown to regard them as the family I never had. But they insisted, pointing out that it was my intervention that had transformed the business from a small, marginally profitable operation into a staggeringly lucrative one in a phenomenally short period of time.''

"So,'' she said, then paused. He could see that she was having difficulty reconciling her thoughts to the idea, but her next words confirmed that she'd gotten the picture. "You're saying that you really are rich."

He lifted a shoulder, thought how best to answer. Finally he decided on the bottom line.

"You could safely say that money is no longer an issue for me."

"And you left it all behind—the business, the Santiagos, a country that you so obviously love—to return to Chicago."

He looked behind him, spotted the wine bottle and snagged it. "I left it to return to my life. The one I haven't finished living."

As he refilled both glasses, she appeared to be struggling with a response, a response that would no doubt point out that the life they'd shared was over. Well, from his perspective, it was far from over. And for sure, he wasn't going to let it be over without fighting the good fight.

With his glass dangling between his fingers, he crossed his legs, drew his heels up under the back of his thighs and fully faced her.

"Tara, Santiago, Inc. is a business. And while I intend to return to Ecuador often—not only to see Vincente and Maria who are very special to me, but to see to the aspects of the business that I can't handle from here—what's most important to me is right here in Chicago. You're here. Brandon is here.

"Look," he said, softening his tone as a cornered expression inched across her face, "I'm not asking you to tell me uncategorically that you're ready to take up that life with me again. But I am asking that you leave some room open to the idea that you owe it—not to me, not even to Brandon—but to yourself to consider the possibility.''

It was that very specific possibility that kept him going when, a short time later, she asked him to take her and Brandon home.

Seven

Later that evening Tara sat across the table from John at a posh but discreet French restaurant. She tried to concentrate on John but she couldn't drag her mind away from the afternoon she and Brandon had spent with Michael.

Not only could she not stop thinking about Michael's reaction to the problems her family and Connelly Corporation were having, she couldn't forget the determination in his eyes, the resolve in his voice.

"It sounds like I have good reason to stay as close to you and to Brandon as I possibly can."

They hadn't argued about it. She'd known it would come to no good end. Besides, Brandon had been getting hungry and a little tired. So she'd let it slide and they'd eaten instead. As promised, they'd had their picnic on the floor, sitting on a blanket, with Lake Michigan spread out below them like a living postcard.

She'd watched in relative silence as Michael coaxed a fussy Brandon into drinking all of his milk and eating his chicken before he could eat his cookie.

Michael was a natural with him. She'd enjoyed seeing the interplay between father and son. All in all, it had been a pleasant afternoon. Brandon had fallen asleep on her lap shortly after eating, and she and Michael had talked about inane things, safe things until she'd thought, rather desperately, that she was so comfortable with him. And then she hadn't felt safe anymore.

She'd felt open and vulnerable and far too susceptible to his charm. To the way he made her want to smile back at him. To the way his dark hair, shorter and tidier than he used to wear it, made him seem so much more mature, so much more responsible, settled. And that made her want to mess that glorious, silky hair with her fingers until a renegade hank of it fell over his forehead as she guided his mouth to hers and let him tumble her to her back on the floor.

She caught herself, manufactured a quick smile and nodded in agreement while John quietly and with total confidence, relayed their selection to the waiter. She had no idea what she'd just agreed to. She had no idea about anything anymore when just yesterday her future had been all but carved in stone.

Then, as now, she hid behind a silence that the uncertainty of the past twenty-four hours had fostered. She sipped her wine. She'd thought she'd known what that future would bring. She would be John Parker's wife, and Brandon would have a father.

But Brandon already had a father. And she was still Michael's wife.

"You're very quiet tonight." John's voice broke through her thoughts.

"I'm sorry." She set down her glass and smiled with apology into the grave solemnity of John's eyes. "I'm not very good company, I'm afraid."

"Paige's return has unsettled you," John said bluntly.

She didn't try to hide her reaction or the small, tight laugh that slipped out.

"That is an understatement of epic proportions."

"You don't have to deal with him, you know. Your father would be more than happy to run interference. For that matter, so would I."

"John," she said kindly, "legally, Michael is still my husband. He will always be Brandon's father. And Michael has been through a very difficult time."

"You still have feelings for him," John concluded at the end of a stoic pause.

"I can't pretend that I don't." She looked at him, then at her hands. "It wouldn't be fair to either of you."

At his prolonged silence, she looked up and into a hurt that she hadn't thought John was capable of feeling. That obvious emotion made it harder to say what she had to say.

"We have a history, Michael and I. We have a child. That doesn't mean I understand what I'm feeling for him now."

Her own words surprised her, sent her into immediate denial. She knew what she was feeling: nostalgia, guilt, regrets over what couldn't be.

John watched her face in the dimly lit restaurant. His emotions once again were tightly concealed.

"And where does that leave us?"

Tara reached for John's hand and covered it with hers.

"You're going back to him," he said.

Soft candlelight flickered between them on the table.

"No," she said quickly, as much for her benefit as for his. "No. I...I'm not going back to him. I intend to follow through with the divorce."

"Then why this indecision where you and I are concerned?"

This was going to be hard. Very hard. She wasn't even sure she herself fully understood the decision she'd come to. She did understand that to continue seeing John would not be fair to him.

Or was it because it wouldn't be fair to Michael? Again, her conclusion surprised her. She'd thought a lot about everything Michael had said, about giving him a chance. About giving *them* a chance.

A chance for what? A replay of what had happened to them before? Before, when they'd been kids? Giving him that chance was like asking her to suspend her memories of those horrible times. It was asking a lot.

And still, here she was, second-guessing herself, agonizing over the possibility that she may have had unrealistic expectations back then. Maybe she hadn't been as proud of Michael for wanting to make his success on his own as she'd claimed. Maybe she'd secretly resented him for not accepting her father's grudging offer to come into Connelly Corporation. It would have been so much easier for them if he had, at least financially.

It would have broken Michael's pride, though, and in the end maybe she'd placed too much blame on that pride. Maybe his pride hadn't been the major factor that had sent their marriage on a downward spiral.

She'd never know now. But she did know what she had to do as far as John was concerned.

"John, while seeing Michael again has complicated things in many ways, it's also clarified some things for me, like *our* relationship."

She stopped while she searched for the best words to say this. Unfortunately, there weren't any best words. There were only true ones.

"What you and I have is special. Very special. It's friendship and caring and yes, I do love you, John."

"But now you realize you don't love me the way you love Paige," he said, preempting her.

She smiled sadly. "Can you honestly say that you're in love with me?"

"Love is a relative term, my dear. But, for the sake of clarity, make no mistake. I am in love with you."

She witnessed the pain in his eyes and realized with some surprise that he really did love her.

"You deserve to have that love returned."

Carefully removing the diamond engagement ring from her finger, she wrapped it in his hand, and held it between both of hers.

"I'm sorry. I'm so sorry I can't be the one to do that."

John slowly withdrew his hand from hers and, without a trace of emotion crossing his dignified and handsome face, dropped the ring into his jacket pocket.

"So, is the wine to your liking?" he asked after a moment as he lifted his glass to his mouth.

It was so like him. Noble, impassive, seemingly impervious to the change she had just leveled on his life. He was backing out. He was backing away. Without a fuss, without one reckless, rash outburst of passion, he was letting her go.

So like John. So unlike Michael.

That was unfair. It was totally unfair to compare John to Michael. It was like equating silk to denim, silver to steel, water to fire. And yet, that's what this all boiled down to. Comparisons. One man to the other. One she did love and wished with everything in her that she didn't. One she didn't love and wanted to.

But she'd experienced Michael's fire; she'd felt the heat of his flame. John was entitled to that kind of reaction from her. It wasn't fair to him that she couldn't give it even though she was resolved to end her marriage to Michael.

Tonight, however, wasn't about Michael. It was about John and what he was feeling. For his sake, she did for him what he'd done for her. She backed gracefully away.

"The wine is wonderful. As are you. Friends?" she asked with both compassion and concern.

"Always." His eyes warmed slightly before he shaded his emotions again. "And as your friend, I'll share a bit of information. Randolph Bains called just before I left to meet you this evening."

Tara felt her stomach dip. Bains was a highly respected and wealthy friend of both John's and her father's. He was also the publisher of the *Chicago Tribune*.

"You're going to pop up on the front page of the society section tomorrow morning I'm afraid. It seems that one of his reporters snapped a photo of you leaving your building today with Paige and Brandon."

She closed her eyes, feeling as bad for John as she felt angry over the invasion of her privacy. Tomorrow it would be a small piece in the *Trib*. The next day the tabloids would run wild with it. She could already envision the headlines when they picked up the story off the wire.

Connelly Heiress Dumps Chicago Tycoon For Long Lost Yummy Hubby

Parker In The Cold As Tara's Hunky Hubby Returns From The Dead To Claim His Wife

"John, I'm so sorry."

He shrugged. "Goes with the territory. Say, I believe I just saw Sam Braxton walk by. If you'll excuse me for a moment, I'll just go say hello."

"Of course."

Tara watched him rise from the table and walk away, this proud and noble man. She'd hurt him. For that she would always be sorry.

She'd also closed a chapter of her life that had just transitioned from a new beginning to yet another unanticipated ending. It should have been harder to do.

It should have been a lot harder.

She was weakening, Michael told himself the next morning as he finished his coffee and scanned the morning edition of the *Tribune*. The picture disturbed him. It had always disturbed him to see his face in print, but it came with the Connelly package. It bothered him more for Tara's sake. She was fair game for any inventive photographer. It was like living in a fishbowl. No privacy. Such was the price of her famous family.

Making sure his cell phone was charged, he slipped it onto the breast pocket of his jacket, snagged the keys to his rental car and closed the door to his hotel room.

The first order of business this morning was to pay a visit to Grant Connelly. As well as things were going with Tara, he was concerned about the information she'd shared yesterday afternoon, specifically, the murder of King Thomas and Prince Marc.

He wanted a word with Grant. He wanted to know if there was more that Tara didn't know. He wanted to know if his wife and son were in harm's way. And then he was going to do everything in his power to reduce any threats of clear and present danger.

His cell phone rang before he even reached his car. It was Vincente—and five minutes into the conversation, he knew he had to make a major change of plans. He only hoped this unexpected turn of events didn't jeopardize the headway he'd made toward winning back his wife.

After a quick, to-the-point discussion with Grant, Michael felt confident that everything was being done to ensure Tara and Brandon's safety. He hadn't earned any points with Grant, the man did not like his methods questioned. Michael didn't care about Grant Connelly's point system. He cared about Tara.

He found her in Brandon's playroom. Ruby had pointed him in the right direction then tactfully left them alone.

It was a sight he'd never tire of seeing—his wife and his child together. Tara sat with her legs crossed in front of her on the floor; Brandon knelt beside her as they made great fun of building towers of blocks then gleefully knocking them down.

His heart did that half-hitch thing it was wont to do every time he saw them together. The thought of leaving them again, if only for a few days, made him physically ill.

"Good morning," he said, standing back in the doorway.

When Brandon spotted him, he let out a happy squeal and scrambled to his feet.

Michael met him halfway, lifting him high in the air before catching his stocky little body against his chest.

"Hey there, big guy."

"Da!" Brandon proclaimed through a drooling grin and clapped his baby hands against Michael's cheeks. "Da. Da. Da!"

"That's right, kiddo. I'm your dad." He shot for light and breezy, but the words came out on a choked whisper.

"And don't you ever doubt it," he added against Brandon's silky hair as he struggled to recover from the pleasure of hearing that one drooling syllable from his child.

He hugged him hard and over the top of his shining head, watched Tara rise and dust off her oatmeal-colored wool slacks. She looked trim and sophisticated in her slate-blue silk blouse that she'd tucked into the waistband and topped with a black leather belt that matched her shoes.

His heart flat-out galloped when he noticed that the diamond solitaire roughly the size of Mt. Everest was no longer wrapped around the ring finger of her left hand.

"Hi," he said, buoyed by the implications, as Brandon, whose tolerance for being held had ebbed, struggled to get down. "You look pretty."

She blushed. He loved it.

"You're looking pretty *GQ*-ish yourself."

He grinned, ran a hand over his tie and squatted down beside Brandon, who was busily stacking his blocks again. The little boy handed him one. Michael placed it on the top of the drunkenly leaning tower.

"What have we got here—a budding architect?"

With another squeal of laughter, Brandon swung his arm through the middle of the stack and sent the whole thing scattering across the floor.

"More like a demolitions expert, I think," she said, shaking her head.

He looked down at the floor, slowly stood. Because he wanted to reach for her, and because her posture relayed uncertainty on her part, he shoved his hands in his pockets.

"There's no easy way to say this," he said abruptly. "I have to leave."

He watched her face, tried to decide if he saw disappointment or resignation. A little of both, he decided and counted himself lucky she didn't just throw him out on his ear.

"I don't want to go. I don't want to leave you. I don't want to leave Brandon. But I don't have a choice."

A quick stab of pain shot through his temple. It had ceased to surprise him two weeks ago but it caught him off balance now. So did the memory of similar scenes in the past. How many times had he said those words to her? *I have to go.* He could see in her eyes that she was thinking the same thing.

"Damn," he swore under his breath, rubbed absently at his temple as the pain subsided. "I hate this. Something came up, something I couldn't anticipate when I left Vincente in the lurch two weeks ago."

Tara's eyes were full of concern, yet she kept her distance. Looking nervous, she walked across the room, picked up one of Brandon's stuffed animals, a soft, fuzzy blue elephant, and held it to her breast.

"Come with me," he blurted out, surprising himself

as much as he'd surprised her. "Come meet the Santiagos. You'll love them. They'll love you and Brandon."

"Michael, I can't just pick up and leave. It's not that easy with a child. I don't even know if my passport is up to date."

"I know." He shot her a crooked grin, trying not to place too much import on the fact that her first impulse hadn't been a flat-out no. Instead, she'd concerned herself with logistics, as if she'd actually considered going before she'd stepped back from the idea.

"It was knee-jerk," he said, running a hand through his hair. "It's just that now that I've found you, I don't want to take a chance on losing you again."

While her face was impassive, her eyes told him that whatever there was between them was a long way from being resolved—and gave him hope that it was a long way from over.

"I'll be gone for three days max," he promised, refusing to be waylaid by her uncertainty. "I know what the root problem is. I can fix it fast.

"Look," he continued when her silence spoke of doubt, "I promise you that this isn't my M.O. anymore. It's just that I left them in a bind."

"Michael, you don't need to explain."

"Yes, I do. I need to make you understand that it's the Santiagos that are important here, not the business. Hell, if it was just business, I'd let things sit on hold forever. But this is *their* business and they're part of my family now. They need me."

Bits and pieces of dialogue from past partings rumbled in the back of his mind like distant thunder, reminders of the many other times he'd left her.

"I need to go, Tara. The company is depending on me."

"And I need you to stay. I need you, Michael. When is it ever going to be about my needs? About what our marriage needs?"

"Go," Tara said, cutting into his regrets, meeting his gaze with a look that said maybe she understood more than he'd given her credit for.

He crossed the distance between them in two long strides and folded her fiercely into his arms.

"Hang in there with me, okay?" he appealed against the silk of her hair. He pulled back, tipped her face up to his. "And hang on to this while I'm gone."

Lowering his mouth to hers, he kissed her with all the passion, all the need and all the hunger that had been building since he'd kissed her yesterday morning in the sunroom.

This time though, he tempered the urgency; this time he controlled the greed.

With a tenderness fostered by her softness, he lingered lovingly over her mouth, asked tentatively for admittance, then melted into her kiss when she opened for him and took his tongue inside.

Tara felt like she was drowning in sensations. That always happened to her when she let Michael get too close. For the life of her, though, she couldn't find it in her to push him away.

She'd missed this. Missed the feel of his big, callused hands holding her to him, pressing her against the growing ridge of his erection, running possessively along her back and hips.

She missed the taste of him on her tongue, the heat of him coiling around her, consuming her with a mind-stealing need to be naked and hot and beneath him.

She was dizzy with it, her breasts aching, her body arching.

"Time out," he managed on a shaky laugh as he dragged his mouth from hers and tucked her head under his chin. "Lord help me, there's nothing I'd rather do than finish this and then start all over again."

He groaned, hugged her hard then swore softly.

"I've got to go, babe. I'll be lucky if I don't miss my flight as it is."

Embarrassed and shaky, she let him set her away.

"You managed to book a flight already?" It was a stupid question, a desperate grab for equilibrium in the world he'd just flipped upside down and was still rocking.

"I finagled a charter. Tara—" He gripped her upper arms. "Think of me while I'm gone, okay? Think of the time we've lost. Think of what we have to gain by seeing this through."

This, meaning them, their marriage.

Suddenly, she was grounded in reality again. She wanted to believe him. She wanted to believe that he had changed, that his priorities had changed, yet the indisputable fact was, he was leaving, like he'd always left.

Where a moment ago she'd been fever hot, she felt a bone deep chill settle in.

"Here."

She looked down as he pressed a key into her palm.

"It's to the condo. Will you work on it for me while I'm gone?"

"Oh, Michael, I don't have any idea how you want it furnished."

"Then decorate it how you want it. If you like it, I'll like it."

She stared from the key to his face.

"Great," he said, squeezing her arms, taking her silence for concession when she hadn't fully processed the implications of his request let alone agreed to it. "I really have to go now."

He kissed her again, swift and hard, and then bent to lift Brandon into his arms.

"You take care of your mother, big guy. And you miss me, just a little, okay?"

"Da!"

"Yeah," he said on a smile and handed Brandon over to Tara. "I'll be back as soon as I can."

With one last lingering look, he turned to leave.

"Michael."

He stopped, stiffened. Tara had the unsettling feeling that he was composing himself before he faced her, bracing for a blow. When he turned back to her, his self-assured smile said one thing. His eyes said another.

His eyes didn't look nearly as sure as he wanted her to think he was. It struck her then, how vulnerable he was. That was a concept that would take some getting used to. The man she'd married had never seemed vulnerable. Invincible, maybe. Determined, absolutely. Vulnerable? Never.

It was that vulnerability that changed her course. Instead of voicing a million reasons why she couldn't and shouldn't work on his condo and that he shouldn't take too much stock in that kiss, she went with her heart.

"About John…"

Dead silence skated on the air between them.

"I want you to know that it's over."

More silence, only this time it was far less tense, far more hopeful on his end.

"It doesn't change things between us," she said gently but without the conviction necessary to wipe away his smile. "I still don't think—"

''Wait.'' He touched his forefinger to the crease of tension furrowing her brow. ''Don't think about what can't be. Don't think about what scares you. Think about this instead. I love you.''

Then he turned and walked out the door.

Eight

"If you really want to divorce Michael, then why have you placed your entire life on hold for the past two years?"

Tara glanced up from her desk at *City Beat*. Her brother, Seth, looking distant and removed in a three-piece power suit, wandered restlessly around her office, his hands shoved deep into the pockets of his trousers.

He was, in short, brooding and he'd evidently decided to take out his dark mood on her.

She sighed and gave him a little slack in that regard. She ached for him, for the turmoil he was going through over his mother. Angie Donahue's sudden return weighed heavily on the minds of all the Connellys. For Seth, however, it wasn't just a weight. It was a blow.

"I thought you came over to take me to lunch, or was that just a ploy so you could pick a fight?" she asked with a narrow-eyed scowl that turned into a grin when he realized he'd been had.

Good, she thought when one corner of his mouth lifted in a tight smile. She was determined to nudge him out of his mood but not at her expense. She had no intention of talking about a topic she simply didn't have it in her to discuss—Michael.

It had been eight days since he'd left for Ecuador with a promise to return in three days. So much for his promises. They meant no more now than they had two years ago. Nothing, it seemed, had changed. He was as driven now as he had been then. And that drive always took him away from her both physically and emotionally. Unless someone had lived it, there was no way to explain the pain that type of isolation caused. But she had lived it. And she couldn't live it again.

Steeped in disappointment and disillusion—she'd actually begun to believe that he'd changed—she fought back her own anger. She was now more cemented than ever in her resolve to go through with the divorce. It was just like she'd told Michael. She couldn't survive him again. Loving him hurt too much.

"I've talked with him you know," Seth said, pausing in his restless prowling long enough to look at her. "Right after he reappeared. The man loves you, Tara. He does not want this divorce."

Tara closed her eyes. Old territory. New route.

"If you don't want to represent me in the divorce anymore, that's fine," she said without heat but with clear resolution. "I'm sure Dad can recommend someone."

He crossed his arms over his broad chest, leaned back against the wall and stared at her long and hard. "You still didn't answer my question."

"What question?" she asked with weary patience.

"If you don't want to be with him, why have you placed your life on hold? You've been waiting for him, Tara. You never gave up on him being alive.

"You love him," he added for emphasis. "There's nothing to stop you from being together any longer."

Nothing but a history of misunderstandings, anger and regret.

She wasn't going to talk about it. Neither would she allow Seth's well-intended meddling to undercut her resolve to be patient with him. He meant well. And he was troubled, now more than ever. She understood that. Just like she'd always understood that Seth, at the core, didn't feel like he belonged with the Connellys. She suspected that was why he was championing Michael's cause now. Michael had never felt like he'd belonged, either. Seth had known that and he sympathized.

Seth was wrong, of course, at least about his position in the family. Their father loved him and her mother had always looked upon Seth as one of her own.

But Tara loved him best of all.

She rose, walked around her desk and hugged him. "I love you, brother mine," she whispered against his ear. "Now back off please or I'll have to get rough with you."

He didn't flinch at her display of affection. Once he would have tried his best to keep an emotional distance from anyone in the family who got too close. Tara had never let him get by with it. She wasn't about to let him get by with distancing himself now.

"Take me to lunch," she ordered, falling into the bossy, bratty little sister role that Seth loved to butt heads with. "And we're going to talk about anything and everything *but* this family and its troubles. Mine included.

"Hey," she said as an idea struck her. "What do you say we take in a ball game? How long has it been since we've watched the Cubs together and fought over peanuts?"

His cool gray eyes warmed as she raised a hand, touched her fingers affectionately to his short brown hair.

"Come on? What do you say? We're due for a little umpire bashing and ketchup stains."

"You always get your way, don't you, brat?" he muttered with a reluctant grin as she snagged her jacket.

"You're just mad 'cause I wouldn't let you bully me. Here's a tip. Get over it."

With her arm linked through his, she dragged him out the door, looking forward to an afternoon where she could feel less troubled and more carefree than she had in a long time. A very long time.

Later that evening Tara sat alone in the den trying to read a book. She finally closed it shut with a snap when she'd had to reread a page three times.

"Go to bed," she told herself. Everyone else had retired over an hour ago, including her parents. Actually, she was worried about her dad. He had a lot on his mind these days. For that matter, they all did.

Except for Brandon. She thought of her son snug and warm in his bed upstairs. He was growing so fast. Sometimes she wished she could lock him on freeze-frame and keep him as innocent and happy and free of the emotional scars life would most certainly give him.

"And how fair would that be?" she murmured aloud. It would be like keeping him from living. From experiencing his own joys and triumphs and, unfortunately, fears. But he would be strong, her son. He would deal with life head-on and come out on top. As a mother, however, she would never overcome her desire to protect, to provide, to harbor.

He asked about Michael every day. Many times. He missed him.

So did she.

And that was one of her greatest fears—that she would never stop missing him.

She dragged a hand through her hair then drew her legs to her chest. Resting her chin on her knees, she stared into the fire. And saw Michael's smoky gray eyes staring back at her. Saw the blue-black highlights in his hair, the unqualified grace of his strong, lean body.

She pressed her forehead to her knees and was reaffirming her conviction that she was better without him when a noise had her lifting her head. She sat very still, listening. It came from outside, like the distant rumble of far-off thunder. She looked toward the window facing the lake, but saw only stars.

The sound grew louder, closer, a deep groundshaking grumble that began to sound suspiciously like a motorcycle.

Tugging her red sweater down over her jeans as she rose, she walked to the front of the house. Ruby met her at the door wearing her robe and slippers.

"What in thunder is all that racket?" Ruby groused around a yawn. Drawing the belt of her robe tighter, she swung open the door.

"Well, for the love of a dangerous man," Ruby said with a gaping grin.

She shook her head, laughed then slid Tara a sly look.

"I don't believe this concerns me. You two have fun now but don't be staying out all night."

Fun? Tara thought incredulously as she stared from Ruby's departing, chuckling form to the sight that met her on the top—the *very* top—step directly outside the mansion's front door.

A leather-clad hooligan straddled the biggest, baddest, loudest motorcycle Tara had ever seen. His black-gloved hands reached to remove a space-aged, lacquered-black helmet, then briskly brushed through hair as dark as the night.

"Hi," Michael said with a tired but broad grin.

Hi? As if he hadn't been gone for eight solid days? As if it was an everyday occurrence that a madman on a motorcycle scaled the twenty-odd steps of Lake Shore Manor at midnight. As if they were still both sixteen and she'd been waiting for him, ready to race out of the house to defy her parents and because there was no place she'd rather be than with him.

Well, she wasn't sixteen anymore. And she shouldn't want to be with him.

But she did.

"It's almost midnight," she said inanely and because she really didn't know what else to say.

She should go back inside. She shouldn't just stand there, her heart beating with excitement and lust for her soon to be ex-husband with the outlaw grin and tight leather pants.

She should go back inside, her mind warned her again, because she was about a deep breath away from throwing caution to the wind, climbing right on the bike behind him and plastering herself as close to him as she could possibly get.

"Yeah. I know," he said above the noise as he

revved the engine with a practiced and competent twist of his gloved hand. The powerful machine responded with a deep, resonating grumble.

She blinked, drew a total blank.

"Know what?" she shouted, then belatedly stepped outside and closed the door behind her in the hope that he hadn't awakened the entire house.

"That it's almost midnight," he said, another grin flashing. "Best time for road-tripping."

"Road-tripping? Michael. You can't just…I can't just…this isn't—"

His white teeth flashed under the porch light. Apparently he was enjoying her incoherent babbling. The soft focused light drifted across his face and a jaw that was lightly shadowed with dark stubble. It made him look as dangerous as the bike—and infinitely more mysterious.

"Come on," he coaxed, twisted at the waist and dug into a black saddlebag trimmed in silver. "It'll be like old times."

He dragged out a jacket that matched his, draped it over her shoulders. Then before she could say yes, no, or this is not a good idea, he eased his helmet over her head.

"You want to come with me," he said with amused certainty. Balancing the bike on strong legs, he helped her work her arms into the jacket sleeves.

"Please?" Watching his hands work from the bottom up, he snapped button after button then tilted her an ornery smile. "Pretty please?"

He fastened the final button under her chin, looked into her eyes—and she was lost.

He used to do this all the time. He used to come for her on his used and rough-running little bike that barely had enough power to climb a hill let alone the steps. And he always had a grin on his face. The same grin he was grinning now.

Dare ya, it said.

His gray eyes beckoned.

When she stood there, torn between a desire to go with him and a common sense that said "no way," he revved the motor so loud she was afraid he'd wake up the entire neighborhood.

She winced and looked toward the closed door.

Rebel that he was, he revved it again.

"Okay, okay," she shouted over the noise and climbed aboard. Then she held on for dear life as they bounced down the steps. "That was nothing short of blackmail."

His voice sounded smug as he shouted over his shoulder. "Worked, too, didn't it?"

Yeah, she thought, giving in to a grin, as they hit level ground and he flew between the open security gates. It worked just fine.

The night was cool and crisp and the longer they rode, the more stars appeared, the brighter was the moon. Tara had no idea where they were going. It frightened her a little that she didn't care.

Her world had shrunk to the sensation of the power of the bike between her legs. Her senses had honed in on the warmth of Michael's broad back seeping through supple leather against her breasts. Her awareness had focused on the assurance and skill of the man weaving at a fast and competent speed through the traffic and away from the city.

They didn't talk. Conversation would have been su-perfluous. This ride wasn't about talking. It was about

remembering and feeling and skating on the sharp, siz-
zling edge of sensation. The sensation of speed. The
impression of power. The awareness of each other.

It would be a disaster to give in to her desire, a ca-
tastrophe to let old memories and rekindled yearnings
team up to weaken her resolve. She couldn't let him
kiss her again. And yet, as they veered off the Sheridan
Road, breezed through Evanston and rolled into a lake-
front park, she tingled with the awareness that it was
exactly what she wanted him to do. And more.

They cruised deeper into the park, closer to the break-
water of Lake Michigan then idled to a stop. Michael
cut the engine, kicked down the stand then swung his
leg over the bike and stood.

The first thing she noticed was the absence of his
body heat against her. The next was that he was watching her. Breakers crashed against the not-so-distant
shore. The wind lifted his hair. The chill in the air made
her shiver. She told herself it was the chill, not the man
who was watching her so intently.

"Like old times, huh?" His voice was gruffly quiet;
his eyes, when he met hers, were seeking. "Bring back
memories?"

Oh yeah. Midnight rides; hot, yearning bodies; wild
wet kisses.

She looked away. "I don't remember that you rode
in this much style back then."

He laughed softly. "You like her?" He lifted a hand
toward the bike. "I placed the order just before I left
for Ecuador. Had to get the dealer to open up after-
hours when I got in tonight so I could drive over."

"You couldn't have waited until tomorrow?"

"No," he said evenly. "I couldn't. Just like I
couldn't wait to see you. I've missed you."

Her eyes must have relayed what she was thinking. He'd missed her so much he'd stayed away five days longer than he'd promised.

"I'm sorry it took so long." He moved a step closer to where she still sat on the bike. "Things got complicated. I called," he said. "You were never home. Or you were unavailable."

He had called. And she had made it a point to be unavailable.

"How's Brandon?" he asked, working off his gloves, one finger at a time.

"Fine. He's fine." She watched his hands, tan and strong as he tucked the gloves in his hip pocket.

"He misses you. He asks about you every day."

"He misses me? Really?"

Such surprised pleasure filled his voice that she smiled. "You've made quite an impression on our son."

"And what about his mother? Have I made an impression on her, too?"

He stood very close now. With moonlight and stars her only light, she could still make out the definition of his broad shoulders encased in the licorice-colored soft leather. She could see the fire in his eyes.

And she knew they were finished talking.

He touched one of those sensual fingers to her jaw, cupped her face in his palm. His gray eyes glittered with longing as he lowered his head.

She could have turned away. She should have turned away and dodged his mouth as she'd dodged his phone calls.

But she couldn't. She just couldn't.

When his lips touched hers, she sighed a little and lifted her mouth to meet him. When his arms banded around her, she died a little and wrapped her arms around his neck.

Heat. Need. Hunger. They spiraled through his kiss as he claimed her. And loss. Aching, yearning loss as his deep groan named her the one, the only woman who could give him what he'd missed. What he wanted. And what he wanted was more. What he wanted was deep, drugging kisses, a connection that went much further than this mating of two mouths in the moonlight on this cold Lake Michigan shore.

"Open," he whispered against her lips. "Let me in. God, Tara, let me in."

With a whimper that could have been protest, or denial or greed, she did as he asked. She opened her mouth, gave in to the need and invited his tongue inside.

Sleek. Silky. Seductive. He thrust and withdrew, pleasuring them both, teasing them senseless. With his mouth still linked with hers, he pulled her off the bike then pressed her back against it with his body.

"So good," he murmured, breaking the kiss long enough to scrape his teeth along her jaw then down her throat before returning to her mouth with an urgency that stole her breath.

And all the while his hands, his big, mobile hands, roamed over her body, pressing her against him, molding her to tight leather and an arousal that pulsed against her belly.

"Touch you," he whispered against her open mouth as he lifted her and set her sideways on the bike. "I need to touch you."

Nudging her knees apart with an impatient hand, he moved between her open thighs, then cupped her bottom and increased the intimacy.

Tara lost herself in his need. It was always like that

with Michael. His hunger took over, sweeping her along in its wake, an eager participant, a wanton respondent in this game he played so well.

His hands were at her throat now, tugging at buttons until her jacket came fully undone. And then they were on her, tunneling up under her sweater, calloused and possessive and lean. He sought her breast, surrounded, caressed her through the silk of her bra.

On a deep groan, he pushed the confining sweater's hem high and lowered his head.

"Michael."

She knotted her hands in his hair, let her head fall back and let herself go. His mouth. Oh, his mouth devoured her. Suckling, licking, tugging and then nuzzling as his fingers moved to her back and flicked her bra fastener free.

She spilled into his hand. He covered her, gently squeezed then lifted her to his mouth again. With the tip of his tongue, he lightly traced her nipple.

She cried out, arched toward him. And then he was suckling her again, with reverence, with such tender attention that she felt the tug between her legs and deep in her womb where her body wanted him to be.

He knew. He knew exactly how to touch her to set her blood burning, to make her yearn, make her beg, make her forget that the communication they'd always shared in bed had never overlapped to the rest of their life.

"Michael," she whispered when his hands and his mouth were on the verge of taking her somewhere she was suddenly afraid to go. "Michael, stop."

"You don't want me to stop." His voice was a deep, edgy whisper as he pressed his hands between her shoulder blades and arched her closer toward him. He languorously bathed her left breast with the tip of his tongue. Then he pinched her nipple between his lips, tugged before lifting his head and seeking her eyes. "I know what you want. Let me give it to you, babe. Let me give us what we both want."

"You're making my head spin."

He chuckled, pressed an openmouthed kiss to the corner of her mouth, scraped his teeth along her jaw line. "Seems to be going around."

"Stop. Michael, please. I can't think when you do this to me."

His mouth tracked kisses along the column of her throat, working slowly, inevitably back toward her mouth. "You don't need to think. You just need to feel." His hands skimmed down her back, cupped her bottom again and pressed her hard against him.

"I do need to think, Michael. Please. I need to think about this a lot."

She felt his big body stiffen. Felt the heat radiate off of him in waves. Slowly, he raised his head, pressed his forehead to hers.

"You're killing me here."

"I'm sorry."

"Oh, babe, don't do that."

He lifted a hand, brushed away a tear. She hadn't even been aware that it was trailing down her cheek.

Then he wrapped her in his arms. "It's okay. I was out of line. It's just...you just..." he paused, laughed roughly. "You make me lose control. You always have. Always will."

He let out a huge breath. "Come on. I'd better get you home while I've still got the will to do it. Besides, I wouldn't put it past your old man to send the cops after me."

"It wouldn't be the first time," she said, managing a shaky smile.

"No. It wouldn't be the first time."

He smiled down at her, his eyes tender. "You can have all the think time you want, okay? As long as you're thinking about me.

"Now let's get you put back together. Turn around."

Like an automaton, she did as he asked, then shivered when his hands tunneled under her sweater again, this time to find the ends of her bra and fasten it for her.

"Okay?"

She nodded.

He brushed a kiss on her forehead then started the motorcycle. The drive home was uneventful, if you didn't count the uneven beating of her heart or her conflicting emotions that waged a war with her common sense.

"Come over to the condo tomorrow morning," Michael said when they'd pulled up in front of Lake Shore Manor.

"Bring Brandon. I need to see him. And I need to see what you've done with the place."

Then he kissed her, a kiss so tender and full of love, she almost cried again.

"Good night, sweetheart," he whispered against her mouth.

She held his gaze for a long, uncertain moment before she slipped inside. Then she leaned back against the door and, for the first time in two years, felt a surge of life. A hope in love. Both were so strong that all of her resolve to stay distant from Michael's charm couldn't wipe the smile off her face.

Nine

Michael was waiting for them at the condo when Tara and Brandon arrived a little before nine the next morning. He'd been up since six. Hell, he'd been up all night—in more ways than one. Thinking of her. Aching for her. Frustrated and encouraged and hopeful in turn.

Last night at the lake...well, he'd hoped the bike ride would set the mood and the stage—a little replay of the stunts they used to pull when they were crazy in love and too young to know any better.

He'd been right. She'd caught the mood and kissed him like he'd been the only man. She'd kissed him like there hadn't been another man in the two years since he'd been gone. And Tara's kisses didn't lie. It only made him ache for her more.

But he tamped down his libido when his doorbell rang and he opened the door to the sight of his wife and his son.

"Da!" Brandon ran into his arms with a squeal.

Michael laughed and swept him into his arms, hugging him hard. "You've sure got that word down pat."

Brandon clung to him like a little monkey. This child's unedited love never ceased to humble him, make him proud, make him strong. Strong enough to win back the woman standing just inside the doorway, her eyes misty with an emotion she couldn't conceal.

"Good morning," he said over Brandon's head.

She nodded, closed the door.

The signals she sent out with a look and the stiff set of her shoulders told him she didn't want to talk about last night. That she needed some distance from what had happened between them—even more distance from him.

Disappointed, but respecting her need for space and understanding that she needed more time to process what she was feeling, he motioned toward the kitchen.

"I made coffee."

See? His smile said. Safe ground. Nonconfrontational.

Instantly, she relaxed.

"It's fresh ground."

"Fresh-ground coffee? This from the man who once lived on instant direct from the microwave?"

He grinned. "I keep trying to tell you, I've changed. I developed a taste for the real thing in Ecuador. Maria makes a mean cup of coffee. I had her teach me."

While Tara shrugged out of her short navy jacket, Michael unzipped Brandon's warm coat all the while taking in her sleek soft body. She'd dressed in narrow denim jeans that molded her slim hips and a snug yellow turtleneck that hugged her lush breasts. He'd always loved her body. He'd finally gotten his hands on it last night, gotten his mouth on her.

He suppressed a groan at the memory and tuned in to her speculative look.

"There's more," she said, her eyes narrowed in hopeful accusation as she lifted her head in the direction of the kitchen area and sniffed. "Something sinful and decadently high cal."

"Guilty as charged. I picked up pecan rolls at the corner bakery while I was taking my morning run."

She arched a brow. "Run? You make time for a run?"

"I make time for a lot of things now," he assured her.

He set Brandon on the floor and poured coffee into disposable cups.

"Some people I know, however—and I'm not naming names here—but some people don't seem to have taken the time to get my furniture or stock my kitchen. All I found when I let myself in this morning were a lot of wallpaper books, color wheels and fabric samples. At this rate I'll never get out of that hotel."

She accepted the coffee along with the smile that softened his scolding.

"Oh, that. Actually, I *have* been busy. I've got an army of retailers ready to deliver truckloads of goods— but they're all on hold. Michael, I couldn't just come in here and dress this place without your input."

"Well, you've got it now. I'm all yours. But first, let's be sinful together. The rolls," he clarified when her eyes flashed nervously to his. "Then—and I can't believe I'm saying this—we'll talk decorating."

That made her smile. He loved her smile. And since

he planned on seeing a lot of her smiles and a lot of her for a very long time, he took the low road.

He didn't push. He didn't persuade. Over coffee, they talked about the weather. They talked about the Cubs and Brandon's favorite toys and favorite food. They laughed at his antics as he alternately stuffed his face with sweet rolls and sipped milk from the ever-present sippy cup his mother had brought along.

In short, they acted like a family, tight, loving and strong.

We can do this. We can *be* this, he told himself with newfound determination as he watched his wife with his son and prayed for the patience and the wisdom to paint himself into this picture with indelible ink.

"You're sure you want blue in here?"

Half an hour later, Tara stood in the middle of what would soon be Michael's bedroom. In her hand was a color wheel. On the floor at her feet were wall-covering books and hundreds of swatches of material. And Michael was watching her with those intense gray eyes and telling her that he wanted blue.

"What's wrong with blue? I figure you can't go wrong with blue, right?"

This from a man who had always radiated red. Or maybe it was her own subconscious working its way into the conversation. Or her memories of last night on his bike, by the lake, when he'd kissed her.

"What? I'm not right? Blue's not good?" Michael asked, reacting to what must have been a puzzled look on her face. If he only knew. She wasn't puzzled. She was pathetic.

She couldn't keep her mind off him. His hands, his mouth, his—

"No," she said abruptly, shaking herself away from the image. "No. Blue is fine. Blue is great. You just…I don't know, I guess you surprised me."

"Because I like blue?"

"Because you would choose blue." She shrugged, shooting for indifference when inside she was so tuned to the rugged strength of his body she thought she'd explode.

He was wearing old, worn jeans today. His sweater was a rich forest-green that somehow managed to deepen the gray of his eyes.

"Why do I get the feeling we're not just talking about a color here?" He tilted his head, eyed her thoughtfully.

"Color preferences sometimes tell a lot about people, that's all," she said, hedging.

"Really. And what does blue say about me?"

Carefully marking the page, she folded the book shut, determined to keep the conversation geared toward decorating. A tough trick considering her thoughts kept sneaking back to the kisses they'd shared in the park.

"Just nothing that I would have associated with you."

He laughed softly. "Now you've got me intrigued. Come on. What does blue say about the person choosing it?"

She hesitated then just said it.

"Well, for one thing, it says that they want to feel relaxed. Blue generally reflects contentment, peaceful moods, tranquil feelings, and that, um, generally reflects the personality of the person who chooses it."

He grinned, looking far too pleased with himself and, she realized, like he was very aware that she was uncomfortable, and why—and that he was enjoying it.

"And you don't think that blue is reflective of me."

Hardly. It was hard to think of Michael in terms of blue when red screamed through her head whenever she looked at him. When the simple action of handing her a cup of coffee and the accidental brush of his fingers across hers sent her heart pounding and turned her knees weak. When she couldn't get out of her mind the picture of his dark head bent to her breast in the moonlight.

"I keep telling you, Tara. I've changed. But, for the sake of argument, you're the expert here, so what color do you see when you look at me?"

She lowered her head, made herself busy gathering up the rest of her samples.

"Black?" he guessed with a smile in his voice when she didn't answer.

Straightening from the stack of materials she'd arranged in a neat little pile, she shoved her hair back from her face with a trembling hand.

"Somewhat. Black exudes discipline, authority, strength."

"But it's not what you'd consider my primary color?"

She wet her lips, very aware that he'd moved to stand directly in front of her. His gaze roamed her face with a tender intimacy that made her shiver.

"No. I wouldn't consider it your primary color."

"What then?"

"Red," she finally said, meeting his slumberous eyes then quickly looking away.

He gently snagged her arm, pulled her toward him until there was little more than a deep breath standing between them.

"What about red, Tara?" he whispered, the promise

of seduction in his voice, as his thumb massaged her upper arm in a slow, sensual caress.

"Red…" She looked up and into his eyes and got lost there. "Red empowers. Red stimulates. Red…symbolizes passion."

His gaze locked on hers, he very slowly walked her backward across the plush carpet. She put up a dismal amount of resistance as his powerful thighs brushed against hers, nudging her along with him, infusing her with aching awareness.

When she met up with the bedroom wall, she went perfectly still. She should stop him. She should push him away. But she held her breath instead, mesmerized by the smoky gray eyes that devoured her.

"*You* empower me." He lowered his mouth, brushed a kiss to her brow.

"*You* stimulate me." His warm breath, scented of cinnamon and coffee, whispered across her face like a caress.

"*You* are every symbol of passion I could ever need." His lips found hers then and she was powerless to turn away.

He slid his tongue along the seam of her lips, coaxing, coercing, promising a pleasure she was so familiar with and so wanted to feel again.

On a surrendering sigh, she opened her mouth, drew his tongue inside, tasting, indulging, loving the feel of him there. And then she simply melted into the erotic heat of his kiss.

She didn't know that she'd raised her hands, tangled them in his hair, didn't feel anything but the sensual sweep of his tongue, his hard body pressing her to the wall.

Sweetly, slowly, and so tenderly that she wanted to

weep, his mouth mated with hers in a thorough, studied exploration as his hips pressed, receded, pressed, telling her how much he needed her. Showing her how much he wanted her.

"Up!"

Brandon's voice came to her from a distance.

"Up! Up! Up!" he demanded, making his presence known not only with his verbal demand, but also with the pinch of his little fingers on her leg.

Michael pulled slowly away, his eyes dark, a soft, indulgent smile on his face. "It appears that somebody's feeling left out."

He kissed her once more, quick and tender, leaving her dizzy. Then he bent down and lifted Brandon into his arms.

"What's the matter, trouble? Am I getting too chummy with your mama?"

Brandon answered with two smacking palms to the side of Michael's face before zeroing in with a wet, sloppy kiss.

"I get it," he said on a laugh. "You want in on the kissing, too."

"Ma!" Brandon said and made a dive for his mother. Together, they caught him. And then he grinned like a little goose, snuggled and secure in the circle of their arms.

Michael lowered his forehead to Tara's, his eyes dancing with contentment, peace and tranquillity.

"Definitely blue," he whispered and she sank into the dangerous sensation of feeling like she was coming home.

Okay, so age hadn't made him wiser, Michael grudgingly conceded. The night was chilly. The moon was high, like a beacon.

"Or a damn spotlight," he muttered under his breath and with a grunt, made a grab for the branch directly above him. When he reached it, got a good hold, he hiked his left leg up and over a higher limb of the tree that grew directly beneath Tara's bedroom window.

He was out of his mind. Love did that to a man. So did lust. She was driving him nuts. For the past several days they'd spent time together, talking, laughing, kissing. Oh, the kissing.

And yet, she held back.

He wanted more. He needed more. And tonight, do or die, he was going for broke. The motorcycle stunt had worked and now he was pinning his hopes that another little stroll down memory lane would work, too.

It had been remarkably easy to slip past the Lake Shore Manor security; he was going to have a talk with Grant about that tomorrow. He didn't, however, remember that this tree used to be such a challenge.

With another grunt, he hauled himself up higher, gauged the distance and made a lunge for the rail. He caught it on the fly and vaulted onto her balcony.

"Still got it," he congratulated himself as he landed on his feet—then caught his breath in a tight little hitch when he saw her.

His heart, already slamming like a sledgehammer, picked up a couple of beats as he stood there, watching her through the glass panes of the French doors.

And suddenly he wasn't thinking about the risk he'd taken coming to her. She was worth every risk. And no amount of second guesses could stop him from thinking about finally having her, skin on skin, heat on heat.

His face was grim as he walked straight to the bedroom door. As expected, the latch was locked. Without ever taking his eyes from the soft, sensuous form asleep on the bed, he reached in the breast pocket of his jacket and pulled out his pick kit.

Just yesterday Ruby had given him the container of personal items Tara had boxed up after his ''death'' two years ago. She hadn't known the kit had been in it. He wasn't proud of the fact that in the most desperate times of his youth he'd used it with a fair amount of regularity—and not just to gain entrance into Tara's room.

''She saved this for you,'' Ruby had said when he'd picked Brandon up for an afternoon in the park. ''Nothing makes me happier than delivering it to you personally.''

And right now, nothing made him happier than to realize the locks on the French doors hadn't been changed. With a soft click, the tumbler gave. Muffling the sound with his gloved hands, Michael turned the knob and pushed.

The door complained softly on its hinges and he stopped, cast a glance toward her bed. When she stirred, then rolled to her side, still asleep, he eased inside.

And stood there, suddenly full of reservations, flexing his hands with uncertainty.

Maybe this wasn't such a good idea after all. Maybe she wouldn't see this as romantic or reminiscent of the passion of their youth. Maybe she'd see it for what it was: a desperate man breaking into her bedroom with every intention of ravaging her.

She stirred again, a restless slide of slim legs against smooth sheets. A gentle fling of an arm above her head as she rolled to her back.

He stood at the foot of her bed, perfectly still but for

the rapid-fire beat of his heart. And then she opened her eyes.

He held his breath.

She blinked once at the ceiling, then again. And then she sat up and looked him straight in the eye.

Astonishment registered first. The round of her eyes, the frantic clutching of the sheet to her breast.

Then came recognition. She reached over and flicked on the bedside light.

"Michael." His name was more breath than substance, more question than accusation as she stared at him in the dimly lit shadows.

"How did you—" She paused, looked from him to the French door that was slightly ajar. "You didn't."

"Um, yeah. I'm afraid I did. Tara, look, this was a bad idea," he said quickly, carefully watching her face. "I went a little crazy." He held up a hand, pleaded with his eyes. "It…it just seemed, I don't know. Romantic, I guess. Like old times, maybe."

He dragged a hand over his face and shook his head. He tried not to think about how her firm, tight nipples pressed against the snug silk of her gown. "Now it just seems desperate."

She was looking at him like she'd never seen him before—or like she never wanted to see him again, he wasn't sure which. He wasn't sure of anything except that he had to get out of there before he made a bigger ass of himself.

"I'm sorry," he said again and lifted his hands in supplication. "Go back to sleep. I'll just go."

He turned to leave, but her soft voice stopped him. "Michael."

He didn't turn around. Couldn't turn around.

"It *was* romantic. It *is* romantic," she whispered.

He did turn then, turned and watched in astonishment as she lay back down on the bed and opened her arms to him.

"Don't go."

He wasn't aware that he'd stopped breathing, hadn't known he was starving for breath the way he was starving for her. He sucked in air on a rush. And yet he held back.

"You're sure?"

"I'm not sure of anything." Her eyes were wide, a little wild, a little desperate as he moved to stand beside the bed.

"Do we have to be sure, Michael? Can't we just act without thinking? Can't we just indulge without guilt?"

"Tara, I want to be with you more than I want to breathe. But I don't want you to be sorry. I don't want—"

"I don't want to analyze this until we're both paralyzed with indecision." There was impatience woven with desperation in her voice.

She sat up and closed her eyes, as if to settle herself down. "You acted on impulse coming here. Let me act on mine. Let this be my dream, Michael. Do you know—you couldn't possibly know—how often I've dreamed of you."

She reached for his hand, slowly pulled off his glove. She kissed his palm, then placed it over her breast.

"Please." There were tears now, warm and glistening as they slid down her cheeks. "Be my dream tonight."

"I don't want to be your dream. I want to be your reality," he murmured as he worked off his other glove then cradled her face in his hands.

"Look at me. Tell me you know this isn't a dream."

"This isn't a dream." She covered his hands with hers. "You're real. Oh, God, you're real."

He cut off her sob with the slant of his mouth over hers, bruising and hard, reckless and greedy. He couldn't help himself. He'd been wanting her for so long, needing her for an eternity.

And when she matched his hunger like a tiger, he forced her to her back on the bed.

She tore at his shirt, dragged it over his head until he wore nothing but a sheen of perspiration.

He rolled with her across the bed, caught up in her aggression, surrendering to his own need. The force of it sobered him. The desperation finally brought him to his senses.

"Easy," he managed on a ragged breath.

He forced himself to settle, forced himself to soothe.

"Easy," he said more sternly and wrestled her to her back again. He dragged her hands above her head, locked them there with one hand as he sat up, his thighs straddling her hips.

With the other hand, he smoothed the hair away from her face and tried to catch his breath and his bearings.

"We need to slow this down, babe. Tone this down or we're going to hurt each other."

She sagged, trembling against the pillow. Her breath was as ragged as his. Her heart beat just as rapidly.

"I just…Michael, I want you so bad."

"Shhh. I know. I know."

He drew another bracing breath, watched the rise and fall of her breasts. "Can I let you go now?"

She nodded, the silk of her hair sliding against the pillow. Slowly, she raised a hand to his chest. Hesitantly, she eased up on her elbows, leaned toward him. He sat rigidly still as she touched her tongue to his shoulder. He sank a hand in her hair when she licked his skin.

"Tara—"

"Let me." She made a sensual, wandering path with her mouth, lapping at his skin, caressing with her lips. She rode the ridge of his collarbone then moved slowly down, until the tip of her tongue swirled with languorous intent at the crest of his nipple.

He groaned, dragged her head back and watched her face, aglow with the power she had over him, sultry with the need to give and take. Only she knew how to drive him wild. Only she knew how to please him.

"I want this off." His hand was shaking as he hooked a finger under the thin strap of her gown and slid it down her arm. Lying back on the pillow, she shrugged the strap off her other shoulder, then helped him shimmy the gown down and over her hips.

"Talk about a dream," he said huskily and stretched out on his side beside her. He traced the cream and honey heat of her with his eyes.

"You are so pretty."

He laid his hand on her thigh, caressed, smiled when she moved into him.

"So pretty."

He couldn't stop looking at her, couldn't stop touching her.

"My turn." His whisper was gritty with need as he lowered his mouth to hers, gently this time, controlling his passion, feeding his desire with tender, lingering kisses to her jaw, to the slender column of her throat. With delicious patience, he kissed the gentle round of her shoulder, lifted her arm and feasted on the silken flesh just inside her elbow.

He couldn't get enough of her breasts. Couldn't touch

them enough, couldn't hold them enough or mold them enough in his hand, in his mouth. Couldn't imagine how he'd lived this long without the gentle weight of them, the resilient softness, the drugging taste.

He nuzzled her under the lower swell, where fragile ribs met luscious heat, ran the tip of his nose around her pretty pink areola, then laved it with his tongue until she moaned.

There was more. So much more that he'd missed about her. So much more he could do to her that would make her quiver and tingle and come apart for him.

He knew what she liked. And she was settled now. Settled and pliant and completely trusting as he slid down her body. He lingered at the sweet indentation of her navel, nipped with a scrape of teeth, a brush of lips at the sharp, slender point of her hip, then indulged in the essence of what made her Tara.

She cried out as he tipped her hips to his mouth. She clutched the sheets in helpless abandon when he parted her feminine folds with his tongue. She groaned his name when he delved deep inside and made slow, intimate love to her with his mouth.

She wasn't the only one who'd dreamed. He'd dreamed of this, ached for this, to hear her sighs, to feel her heat, to taste her release as she stiffened, shuddered and shattered. For him. Only for him.

He raised his head, pressed a kiss to the inside of her thigh, then watched her drift, witnessed her glide in the tingling aftershock of the pleasure he gave, the love he made.

"I love you," he whispered, in awe of her sensual release. He positioned himself between her thighs, bit back a groan as the moist tip of his sex nudged her there, where she was wet for him, ready for him.

"I love you," he repeated as he eased into her tight, sheathing heat and she took him in.

With her arms around his back, her sleek legs wrapped around his hips, she took him deep, guided him to that place where nothing existed but him and her and the incredible rush of losing himself inside of her again.

Ten

—————

Tara leaned against the headboard of her bed, the corner of a sheet wrapped around her to ward off the chill, her arms wrapped around her knees. And she watched her husband sleep.

He lay on his stomach, spread-eagle across the center of the bed, his dark hair mussed, his body limp and sated. He was so beautiful.

She wanted to touch him again. She felt like she'd never get enough of touching him. But she held back. Let him sleep.

It was close to morning. They'd made love all night long. Hot and hurried. Slow and languorous. Intense and demanding.

It had been incredible. It had been wonderful.

It had been a horrible mistake.

She'd given herself to him completely, let him break

down all of her barriers and bare her soul in the ultimate act of intimacy.

And where did that leave them now?

It was so easy when they were together like this. Naked. Vulnerable. Completely trusting each other with their bodies, but not their thoughts.

That had always been part of the problem—they'd used sex as the cure.

And it scared her. She'd just given herself over to him. The love she felt was so powerful. She'd lost herself in it once. She was afraid of losing herself again.

"Hi."

Her gaze connected with his in the pale light of a slow-breaking dawn.

"I didn't know you were awake."

"You okay?"

She looked away. He wasn't having any of it. He raised up on an elbow. "Come here. Come here to me."

Telling herself that she shouldn't, knowing that they should talk, she still took the coward's way out. She let him pull her down into the warmth he offered, let him wrap himself around her back, let him find the heat of her, the need in her, let him take her to that place where nothing mattered but the moment and the pleasure and the need.

Flat on his stomach, Michael eased awake by inches. He felt wasted yet reborn as he burrowed deeper in Tara's bed, savoring the scent of her and of sex and of a morning that glistened with sunlight.

He stretched out the kinks then rolled to his back, disappointed but not surprised that she was gone. They'd made love all night and here he was, wanting her again.

He gave a moment of thought to whether he should just get dressed then leave the same way he'd come in or walk down the stairs like he belonged here. In the end, he decided that after last night, there couldn't be any question that he belonged.

She'd surrendered to him. In every way. Body, heart, soul. He couldn't wait to talk to her, to start making plans for the three of them to be together again.

He already had it figured out. They could live in both Chicago and Ecuador. She was going to love it there. The Santiagos would love her. And Maria—Maria was going to melt into a puddle on the floor when Brandon opened up his arms to her with that joyful infectious grin.

He actually found himself singing as he showered in her bathroom, then grinning as he opted out of shaving when all he found were fragile pink razors that probably wouldn't skim the fuzz off a peach. Although, he thought with a smile as he stepped into his jeans and zipped them, her legs had been as smooth as silk against his back, against his mouth.

"Shake it off, Romeo," he muttered. "Get yourself downstairs and find your woman."

Deciding he was as presentable as he could make himself, he opened the door and walked into the hall. All was quiet upstairs so he descended the grand staircase and followed his nose to the family dining room.

Emma looked up then masked her shock with a warm smile when she saw him hesitate in the doorway. "Well, this is a nice surprise. Good morning, Michael."

"I hope I'm not intruding," he said, unable to suppress a smile.

Grant looked startled, then resigned. Eyes fixed on Michael's face, he lifted a cup of coffee to his mouth.

"Ruby," he said, after a sip, "looks like we need another place setting for breakfast."

Not exactly "Welcome back to the family, son," but it was a start.

"I'll get on that right away," Ruby chirped and tossed a wink over her shoulder as she bustled into the butler's pantry.

"Da!"

"How ya doing, buddy?" He crossed the room to his son, who sat in his high chair like it was a throne and he was lord and supreme ruler of his domain. "Pancakes, huh?"

"Um," Brandon mumbled and forgoing his spoon, shoveled a big bite of a syrupy cake into his mouth.

"Maybe *you* can teach the boy some manners," Grant grumbled with a frown that immediately melted to an indulgent smile when his grandson turned his irresistible grin his way.

Michael was still absorbing the implications of Grant's grudging acceptance of his unannounced presence when Tara walked into the room, a wet washcloth in hand.

"Here you go, Bran. Let's get some of that syrup off your fingers, okay, baby?"

She stopped short when she saw Michael.

There was that blush again.

"Good morning," he said.

"Um. Good morning," she said, regaining her composure, but not her natural color.

"I hope this is okay," he said carefully, watching her face for any sign that she felt as reborn and renewed as he did after their night together.

He saw only nerves, recognized a tension in her body

language that said she had closed off again, shut him out again. It hurt that she wouldn't look at him.

Okay, he thought rationally. This was awkward for her. He could understand that. Maybe. Or maybe not after everything they'd shared last night.

A tightly coiled anger had him clenching his jaw. Maybe he should have just left. Maybe he shouldn't have come in the first place.

And maybe you should just put yourself in her shoes and realize that she took a major step toward you last night when she could have shoved you away.

Yeah. Maybe, he decided and settled himself down.

God, she was beautiful. He wanted to talk to her. He wanted to tell her that he understood—at least he was trying to. That he was willing to give her time.

But that wasn't destined to happen. At least not this morning.

"Call for you, Mr. Connelly," Ruby said as she entered the dining room, a portable phone in hand.

"Connelly here," Grant said, his coffee cup in midair. "Oh, Lord."

Michael looked across the table at his father-in-law. His face had drained to pale. He suddenly looked ten years older than when Michael had walked into the room less than five minutes ago.

Grant set the cup down heavily on the table and slumped back in his chair. "Yes. Yes. I can be there. Thank you."

He punched the disconnect button, heaved a breath that held the weight of the world.

"Grant?" Emma reached over and covered his hand—a hand that was visibly shaking. "Darling, what is it? What's happened?"

"It was the police. There's been another murder."

"Oh my God," Emma murmured. "Not one of the children, Grant—"

"No. Oh, no, darling," he quickly assured her. "It's...it appears to be Tom Reynolds," he said bleakly.

"Of Rey-Star?" Michael put in, recalling Tara's accounting of the private investigation agency Grant had hired.

"Yes," Grant said grimly. He looked across the table at Michael, then slowly moved his gaze to his wife. "I have to go. I have to go down there."

Emma closed her eyes, turned her hand into Grant's when he laced his fingers with hers. "How?" she asked. "What happened?"

Grant shook his head. "I don't—they didn't—aw, hell, I don't know anything. They asked me to come down to police headquarters and identify his body."

"Oh, Daddy." Tara's eyes were glassy with shock and sorrow. "I'm so sorry."

Grant pushed slowly away from the table, stood on wooden legs. "Please just have Ruby order a car brought round." He dragged a hand to his hair, clearly shaken.

"Let me take you, sir," Michael offered.

He didn't add that he didn't think Grant was capable of doing this on his own in his present state.

The older man glanced up, his eyes relaying gratitude. "Fine. Yes. That'll be fine."

"I'll come, too." Tara stood, placing a supporting arm around her father's shoulders.

"No," both men said in unison.

Their eyes connected across the room, an acknowledgment of this rare moment of agreement between them.

"Stay here, Tara," Michael said gently. "Stay with your mother and Brandon."

He didn't want to leave her. He wanted to stay with her, talk about last night, talk about their future. But that had to take a back seat for the moment.

"Come on," he said, a hand at Grant's elbow. "We'll walk to my car. It's parked just outside the gates."

The short walk would do him good, Michael decided. Grant needed the fresh air, needed the time to stabilize, to gather himself.

On the grim ride to police headquarters Michael listened as Grant took him into his confidence and talked out his anger and grief. He talked about the investigations, about the integrity of Tom Reynolds, a man Grant respected and liked.

And Michael listened, letting himself be a sounding board. Grant needed to vent. He needed to rage. And for the first time since he'd known him, Grant had needed him. Had accepted him.

That acceptance served to strengthen Michael's resolve to save his marriage and resume his place in the Connelly household, not as an outsider looking in, but as a member of the family. A member that Grant Connelly could count on to not let him down.

Michael had to give the older man credit. He stood strong in the face of death.

They had just left the morgue after Grant had given the police a positive ID on Tom Reynolds when a lovely young woman with shoulder-length, tawny brown hair and beautiful chocolate-brown eyes met them in the hall.

Her pocket badge identified her as a detective with the Special Investigation Unit.

"Grant." She folded him into her arms. "I just heard. I got here as soon as I could."

Grant hugged the younger woman hard, then set her away. "They killed him. The bastards killed Tom Reynolds."

"I know," she said gently. "I'm so sorry."

Michael stood back, not wanting to intrude on what was obviously a close relationship.

"I'm sorry," she apologized, finally noticing Michael. She searched his face as if she thought she should know him. "I'm Elena Connelly, Grant's daughter-in-law."

"Brett's wife," Michael concluded with a friendly smile and extended his hand. "I'm Michael Paige." Michael knew she'd recently given birth and hadn't yet returned to work. Her efforts to be here for Grant spoke volumes about her affection for her father-in-law.

"Michael, I'm so glad to finally meet you. I only wish it could have been under better circumstances."

"What's happening, Elena?" Grant interrupted, dragging himself out of his shock. "Who killed Tom?"

"They don't know. What they do know is that he was killed in the back alley behind Broderton Computing."

"Broderton?" Grant frowned. "That's the firm Charlotte hired to repair our computer system. In fact it was Charles Broderton himself who did the work. Said he didn't want to trust it to one of his technicians."

"Yes. We know." Elena steered him calmly down the corridor and toward a bank of offices wedged around a main booking area. "And they're already looking at the connection. Why don't you have a seat here in the hall?''

Grant stopped abruptly, craning his neck. ''Wait, that's Charlotte.''

Michael turned his head in time to see the woman he recognized as Charlotte Masters, Grant's executive secretary, being escorted into what appeared to be an interrogation room.

''Charlotte!'' Grant shouted and bolted toward her.

The young woman turned away, her posture one of abject defeat, and allowed the detectives to guide her into the room.

With a look, Elena begged Michael to help her contain Grant.

''Hold on, Grant,'' Michael urged, pressing a firm hand against his chest. ''I'm sure there's a logical explanation.''

''Unfortunately, I'm afraid it's beginning to appear all too logical,'' Grant said sadly.

Michael glanced toward the closed door behind which the detectives held Charlotte Masters. She'd looked pale and shaken. Michael figured maybe he'd look the same if he'd been responsible for hiring a computer tech and then the detective investigating the case turned up dead right outside the tech's firm.

''I want to be in there when they talk to her,'' Grant demanded. ''I insist on being in there. I want to get to the bottom of this.''

''Please, Grant, stay here with Michael. Let me see what I can find out, okay?''

Grudgingly, Grant settled into a chair. When Elena came back a few minutes later, Grant sprang to his feet.

''It's a no go,'' Elena said, her face grim. ''I can't

even get in on the questioning because officially I'm no longer on the case.''

"That's ridiculous! You've been on this case since the beginning.''

"But I'm not on it now and officially I'm still on maternity leave,'' she pointed out. "Please. You're not doing anyone any good here. Go on home. I'll find out what I can and come over to the house later, okay?''

Clearly, it wasn't okay.

"Come on, Grant.'' Michael put a hand on his arm. "Elena's right. There's nothing you can do here. As soon as she knows something, so will we.''

Later that afternoon, however, when Elena stopped over at Lake Shore Manor, they didn't know anything more than they had that morning.

"They've sealed Charlotte's testimony,'' she said gravely as Emma and Grant along with Tara and Michael sat in the den.

"What does that mean?'' Grant pressed.

Elena drew a hand through her hair. "It means that only the detectives currently involved in the case have access to what she's told them.

"My best guess, however,'' Elena continued, "is that Charlotte may have implicated Angie Donahue because shortly after they talked to Charlotte the detectives picked up Angie for questioning.''

"Angie Donahue?'' Michael held up a hand. "Wait—I feel like I've walked into the middle of a movie here. What does Seth's mother have to do with any of this?''

Everyone in the room waited in tense silence for Elena to fill in the missing pieces of the puzzle.

"Angie's father is Edward Kelley,'' she said and let the information sink in.

"Kelley," Michael mused aloud, a frown creasing his brow. "As in the Chicago Kelleys?" he asked, incredulous as recognition dawned.

Elena nodded grimly.

"Oh man. You're talking organized crime here. Organized crime that's as big and bad as it gets. And you're thinking the Kelleys may ultimately be behind—" he stopped, not wanting to voice what he was thinking. "Behind what exactly?"

"Well, now that Angie's connection to the Kelleys has been brought to light, we're figuring they're behind basically everything," Elena said. "From King Thomas and Prince Marc's deaths to the attempt on Daniel's life after he launched the audit on the Rosemere Institute and most recently to Tom Reynolds's death.

"I'm so sorry, Grant, Emma." Elena turned to her in-laws, her eyes filled with sympathy.

At Michael's look of confusion, Tara explained. "The Institute was founded a few years ago after my grandmother, Queen Lucinda, died of cancer."

"Go on, Elena, please," Grant said, looking like a man whose world was falling apart around him.

Elena shook her head. "I'm sorry, Grant, but I don't have anything more of substance to share with you. Angie lawyered up once she realized she'd already said more than was wise for her health. Everything from this point on is speculation."

"My God. You mean they—the Kelleys—might kill her, too?" Emma's face had drained to chalk.

"Her father would try to protect her, I'm sure, but he'd have to contend with Franklin Kelley—and if our conclusions are right, Franklin is behind three deaths already and the failed attempt on Daniel.

"In any event," she continued after a painful silence,

"we have to be thinking the worst—with Angie's connection to the Kelleys—the fact that it was Angie who told Charlotte to recommend Broderton to Grant to repair Connelly Corporation computers and now, Tom Reynolds murdered behind Broderton's—well, there's something more afoot than we'd ever suspected."

"How much worse could this get?" Emma said sounding horrified.

"Much worse, I'm afraid," Elena said on a heavy sigh. "Obviously it was Charlotte who gave the police the information to implicate Angie because it was right after Charlotte's interview this afternoon that they brought Angie in."

"And that makes Charlotte the Kelleys' next target," Grant stated, his tone filled with abject defeat.

Elena crossed the room, took Grant's hands in hers. "As Charlotte was leaving headquarters, a sniper with a rifle took a shot at her."

Emma gasped.

Grant swore.

"She wasn't hurt, fortunately. After the incident, she agreed to cooperate with the police and to accept their protection."

"Where is she?" Grant said. "Where are they keeping her?"

He stopped short, then went ashen when he saw the look on his daughter-in-law's face. "What?"

"She asked to go to her apartment to pick up some clothes and personal items. While our man was waiting for her in the unmarked, she slipped away from him."

Tara glanced at Michael who shook his head. This was not looking good for Charlotte.

"What do you mean, slipped away?"

"She's gone, Grant. She ran. We've got as much

manpower as we can afford looking for her but it was three hours ago and she's just plain disappeared.''

"Your father's pretty much devastated.''

Michael watched Tara carefully later that evening. She clutched a wineglass in her hand as they sat alone in the den, finally. He'd been trying to get her alone all day. She'd managed to avoid that until now. But now the entire house had gone to bed and she was literally forced to face him alone.

She'd been playing with her wine more than sipping it, Michael noticed. He hadn't done much better with his own glass, fighting an encroaching sense that all was not as right with his world as he had thought.

He watched her carefully, watched and waited for some sign, some reason to make him think that true healing had begun last night. That they had finally found their way back to each other.

"This doesn't look good for Charlotte,'' he offered up as a way to break her silence.

"It's so hard to believe she has anything to do with this mess,'' she said at last. She pinched her lips between her teeth and shook her head. "Dad practically views her as one of the family.''

"What about Tom Reynolds's partner?'' Michael asked, unable to keep his mind from straying back over the events of the day even though what he wanted to do was talk about the two of them and where they went from here. "Where does Lucas Starwind fit into this?''

"He was called out of town on a personal emergency not long ago. He'd given Dad a number to reach him before he left so Dad was able to reach him this afternoon and tell him about Reynolds.''

"Must have been hard.''

Tara nodded. "The two men were close. Dad said that Starwind's stone-cold silence on the other end of the line was very unsettling."

After a lengthy and troubled silence, Tara rose, walked to the fire. "Dad put in a call to Rafe this afternoon."

"Where is he?"

"Arizona, I think." She pressed the wineglass against her temple as if to soothe an ache that had settled there. "Some big software project he's been wrapped up in for Connelly Corporation."

"I take it he won't be wrapped up in it much longer?"

She smiled tightly. "Dad told him to get his tail home pronto. He needs someone he can completely trust digging into those computers to see if Broderton corrupted them in any way. That someone is Rafe."

"Grant's right," Michael agreed. "He does need someone he can trust."

It didn't take a rocket scientist at this point to put two and two together. With Angie's connection to the Kelleys, the fact that she told Charlotte to recommend Broderton to repair them, and now Tom Reynolds murdered behind Broderton's—well, there was something bigger afoot here than even Michael had first suspected.

"Dad has never wanted to believe the worst of Charlotte," Tara said, interrupting his thoughts, "None of us have. But what choice does he have? And now that she's disappeared..." her thoughts trailed into silence.

Michael thought of the tall, slender strawberry blonde. Personally, she'd always seemed like a cold fish to him. Cool, reserved, standoffish. But Grant Connelly had trusted her. That had to count for something. He hoped for everyone's sake that she would turn up soon and either clear her name, which had gotten muddied up pretty badly with the disappearing act she'd pulled today, or shed some light on a situation that was growing more volatile by the moment.

"Come with me to Ecuador," he blurted out before he fully thought it through. After he'd said it, however, he knew it was the right thing to do. He had to get Tara away from here. He had to get her alone, get her away so they could build on the foundation he'd been laying the past week and then cemented last night.

"Michael—"

"You and Brandon," he interrupted, warming to the idea. "Don't say no this time, Tara. I don't like what's happening around here. I don't like to think of you in the line of fire of some plot or whatever the hell is going on that involves murder and missing persons."

She looked from him to her wine. She was afraid to go with him, he realized. More afraid of being alone with him than staying here and facing this deplorable situation.

"We owe this to each other, Tara. What happened between us last night—"

"Was physical," she said quickly. "It was sex."

If she'd hurled a rock and struck him in the chest, she couldn't have inflicted sharper pain.

He looked at her as if she'd just arrived from another planet. A cold, black dread seeped into his chest and spread. Anger, deep and disturbing, joined his railing emotions. "Excuse me? I was there, remember? That wasn't just sex. That was— For God's sake, Tara. I was the one whose name you were calling. I was the one—"

"Michael, sex was never our problem."

He couldn't believe she was reducing what happened between them last night to sex.

And that was when it hit him. If last night hadn't convinced her, then he wasn't going to win this fight. There wasn't enough of the old Tara left in her to want to make it work.

And yet, the part of him that would always love her, would always want her, had him butting his head up against that brick wall one more time.

"So let's talk about our problem," he ground out, his teeth clenched against a reality he'd been foolishly determined to ignore—just like he ignored the sharp stab of pain pulsing at his temple. "Oh no, that won't work, will it? Because it takes two to talk, and it's damn hard to talk when you always run away."

She met his eyes warily. She had nothing to say. No denial. No plea for understanding. And it was her silence, echoing with apathy, that finally had him tossing in the towel.

"God, Tara. What else can I do? I've told you I've changed and you choose not to believe me. I ask you to open up and you shut me down like a damn cell phone. Click. Problem solved."

She pinched her eyes shut, then turned her back on him. "I think you'd better leave now."

He shook his head, hung his hands on his hips and looked at the ceiling in utter defeat.

"Yeah," he said, fatigue weighing him like lead. "I think I'd better. I'm wasting my time here. I give up, okay? I give up. On us. On you. Because, you know what? You were right. You're *not* the same woman I married. That woman was a fighter. That woman was passionate about what she wanted and who she loved.

"That woman," he said with a weariness that had settled so deep he felt the ache in his bones, "is gone. She's the one who 'died' two years ago, not me."

The room had grown eerily quiet. Only the fire in the fireplace crackled softly. Above it, he heard the thunder of his blood pounding through his ears.

''I don't like this woman who took her place. This woman's a coward. This woman believes that what happened between us last night was sex.

''The woman I married, the woman I loved, knew the truth. The woman I married knew that every time I held her, every time I made love to her, I was giving her a piece of my soul.''

He walked away from her to the door, all fight gone, all passion bled out of him as surely as if she'd fired a shell and hit him straight in the heart. And even then, he waited. Waited for denial, for her tears. For anything that would tell him he was wrong. But he wasn't wrong, not about this. ''I won't contest the divorce,'' he said at last. ''All I ask is liberal visitation with Brandon. Your attorney can reach me in Ecuador. I'll get the address to you tomorrow before I leave.''

He stopped with his hand on the door handle, waited several heartbeats and turned back to her.

Her head was down. She appeared to be trying to hold herself together by banding one arm around her waist; the other covered her mouth. Twin tears trickled down her cheeks.

''It could have been so good.'' He looked at the face he loved one last time then turned and walked away from her—and from the life he'd lost for a second time in as many years.

Eleven

"In the upper plateau country, the people have a saying," Maria said in her carefully spoken English as she walked to Michael's side.

He sat on the veranda, sprawled in a patio chair. He'd just come in from the forest after another twelve-hour day in a string of twelve-hour days.

He loved Maria, but all he wanted to do was nurse his beer and the sour mood that had settled and held since he'd returned from Chicago two weeks ago. If he couldn't erase Tara from his mind, then his plan was to work himself to exhaustion so he wouldn't have the strength to even think about her.

So far, it was a lousy plan, except for the fact that he didn't have those infernal headaches anymore. Evidently when he gave up on Tara, it was the equivalent of ceasing to bash his head up against a brick wall.

He wiped the back of his wrist across his forehead,

catching the stream of sweat that trickled toward his jaw.

"The people in the upper plateau always have a saying," he said with weary affection, feeling guilty for the concern darkening her eyes.

"They say," she continued, undaunted, "that a man can experience all four seasons in only one day in Ecuador."

Michael lifted the bottle to his lips, set it down and resumed his vacant stare across Maria's gardens, where the setting sun set her tropical plants shimmering with color and life.

Four seasons in a day. Hell. He felt like he'd lived four lifetimes, let alone four seasons since he'd left Chicago and Tara two weeks ago. Four long, empty lifetimes.

"Mornings are warm, like summer," Maria continued in her soft, lilting accent that was rich with her Central American heritage. "Noon is like springtime, because the sky becomes overcast. Afternoon is fall, cool with rain. And night is like winter, cold and luminous."

She sat down beside him and ran her hand in a maternal caress along his cheek. "I fear that your days have all turned into but one season, Miguel. Your heart is cold, always cold like winter."

Since he'd returned to the Santiagos, he'd gotten past listening for the phone to ring, for a little boy's laughter, a light footstep, an indication that Tara had found that part of herself she was missing and had come to him.

It wasn't going to happen.

In the meantime, his life would go on. Somehow.

"I'll be all right." He forced a smile for the dark

eyes that had been pinched with concern and sorrow ever since he'd returned.

"You would be better, no, if summer comes into your life again?"

Summer meaning Tara.

"Yeah, well, I don't think that's something I'm going to hold out a whole lot of hope for."

"Not even if I ask you to give me another chance?"

His heart slammed him hard, once, then several times in succession.

He glared at the nearly empty bottle of beer. Told himself that maybe he'd been hitting it a little too hard.

"We're worth another chance, don't you think?"

Tara.

He closed his eyes, swallowed, too full of wanting to believe he'd actually heard her voice. Too drained of hope to accept that it could be true.

But when he opened his eyes, it was to Maria's encouraging smile—and then to the sight of Tara's face as she walked into his field of vision, looking more beautiful than he'd remembered, more fragile, and yet, somehow filled with resolve.

Maria squeezed his hand then rose. "Summer, Miguel. I think it has arrived." Then she left them.

He didn't know where to look, in the end, he settled on her face—her beautiful cherished face that held a world of uncertainty and a smile so tentative and sweet, something in his chest tightened, knotted.

"You were right," she said, taking a hesitant step toward him. "It is very beautiful here."

She wore a soft, willowy sundress in muted colors of the rain forest, subtle greens, pale lavender, iridescent peach. A breeze molded the filmy fabric to her gentle curves.

"You look like a flower," he said gruffly and rose as she extended her hand.

He took it, resisted the urge to pull her into his arms and hold her.

"I didn't know how to handle it," she said without preamble. She stared at their linked hands, then met his eyes. "I didn't know how to handle all of the feelings. There were so many, Michael. There *are* so many."

She touched a hand to his face, then withdrew it, looking suddenly vulnerable again.

"That woman? The one I'd become? The one you didn't like? I didn't like her, either. But it took you leaving to make me see her for what she was. She was a coward. Too much of a coward to let herself believe in her feelings. Too much of a coward to believe in you."

"What happened to her?" he asked gently as his heart tripped over itself with love.

"I gave her the boot," she said with some of her old fire. "Someone that pathetic—well, she wasn't someone I wanted to associate with any longer."

For the first time since he'd seen her standing there, he let out a breath that didn't feel like it was choking him.

"What finally made you see her for what she was?"

Her beautiful violet eyes searched his face as if she were memorizing it. She lifted her hand, traced his jaw with her fingertips.

"Well, I took a good long look in the mirror one day and realized I could no longer tell her from me."

He caught her hand and pressed it against his mouth. "And now you can?"

"Now I can. In her defense," she said, melting into

the arms he opened for her, "she was dealing with some pretty heavy fears."

He tucked her head under his chin, pressed his lips to her hair. "Tell me about them."

"To begin with, she was afraid to believe you'd really changed, so afraid that she didn't recognize the changes you showed her every day, in so many ways.

"And then there was her fear of being exposed as a hypocrite."

"Hypocrite?"

"She was afraid you'd figure out she was the one who was afraid to communicate even as she told herself it was you who never opened up.

"And she was afraid of the strength of the feelings she had for you," she added against his chest. "Two years, Michael. For two years she'd blocked and dodged and denied the grief. It hurt too much to let herself feel."

"Even love," he finished for her.

"Even love," she echoed and pulled away far enough to look into his eyes.

"Losing you hurt so much, Michael. And I—she—she'd lost you twice, don't you see? Once when she thought that divorce was the only option, and again when she thought you were dead."

"And then I came back from the dead," he concluded, as understanding dawned.

She nodded. "And when you did, she was so…I can't even explain how it made her feel. She wanted so badly to love you, but she couldn't. She simply couldn't work up the courage to risk it—"

"Because she was afraid she'd lose me yet again," he interrupted.

Tears welled in her eyes. She bit her lower lip, nodded. "She wasn't very brave, was she?"

He gathered both of her hands in his, pressed his lips to her knuckles, lingered there. "Maybe she was just confused."

"That, too," she said on a quick burst of sound that was more a release of tension than laughter.

"I guess it's not so hard to understand why she was afraid, is it?" he said, bringing her hands to his shoulders, letting her know he did understand.

"No. I guess it's not so hard to understand. I'm finding it a little hard to forgive her, though. She almost let her fear get a hold of me. She almost made me let you walk away."

"Almost." He lowered his head and kissed her then, because he just couldn't not kiss her. "Almost—that's a word I can deal with so much better than never. As in never seeing you again."

Her eyes glittered with unshed tears. "Never's not such a bad word when it's put in proper context."

"For instance…" He scattered kisses to her face, her jaw, returned to her mouth and started all over again.

"For instance, I've never loved anyone the way I love you. I've never believed there was anyone on this earth who could love me the way you do.

"I'm never going to stop loving you, Michael. I'm never going to let you leave me again. And I'm never letting that woman back in our life. I can survive anything as long as it's with you."

Moonlight washed over the rumpled sheets and the man who lay on his back across them—golden tan, muscled and lean.

Tara knelt over him, straddling his lap, loving the

way he looked at her, shivering with banked pleasure as he lazily lifted his hand and traced his finger lovingly around her areola.

"Look at you," he whispered when her nipple crowned.

Her back arched toward him, an involuntary response to his merest touch.

"Look at how pretty you are. Come here to me."

He raised up on his elbows as she rose to her knees, leaned toward him, offering her breast. And then his mouth was there, laving, licking, tugging with gentle suction then ravenous greed.

She pulled away and his mouth followed. She laughed, low and sensual, as he fell back, a smile so utterly male, so erotically pleased that she caught her breath.

"Feeling frisky, are you, Mrs. Paige?"

"Feeling strong, Mr. Paige," she countered huskily as she wove her fingers with his, stretched his arms up and over his head, brushing her breasts provocatively against his chest—for the pleasure of it, for the triumph of it, for the thrill of seeing his eyes darken to smoky cobalt.

"You're playing with fire here," he warned as he turned his head, caught the tender flesh of her shoulder in his teeth. "And you're gonna feel the burn."

"I'm already burning," she murmured, releasing his hands and running her fingers in a slow, sensual caress along his arms until she reached his chest. There she lingered, tracing the contour of sculpted muscle with her fingertips, then with her tongue.

"Tara," he uttered on a groan as she worked her way slowly down his body, the brush of her lips, the flick of her tongue, the nip of her teeth.

"I love you, Michael," she whispered as she moved lower, took him in her hands, caressed, adored, then took him in her mouth. "Love you, love you, love you…"

And when it was over, and they lay gasping for breath and tangled in each other's arms, she looked into his eyes and told him the way it would be. "I'm never going to stop loving you. I'm never going to leave you. I'm never going to let you go away from me again. Never."

And he smiled, because there, under the light of the Ecuador moon, in this exotic place where he'd once been lost, he found himself. He found his wife. And because he knew that never was a long, long time.

The whole family turned out. Even Vincente and Maria made the trip from Ecuador to Chicago for this special day. Maria held a lace hankie to her trembling lips and dabbed at her tears—she was such a romantic.

The day was benevolent and warm, the breeze only slight. Mums in every color imaginable adorned the altar and the aisle as Tara and Michael renewed their vows in the garden at Lake Shore Manor.

And Brandon, in his knee britches, jacket and tie, kept everyone in stitches as he played peekaboo around his mother's legs until his father, with a barely suppressed grin, lifted the little boy up and into his arms so they could finish the ceremony.

"This is a little different from the first time around," Michael whispered in Tara's ear as they stood in an informal receiving line and accepted the congratulations of Tara's family after listening to Grant Connelly offer a moving and heartfelt toast to the bride and groom.

Tara slipped her arm around his waist. "The first time was still more fun," she said with a teasing grin.

"I love you," he whispered as he bent down to kiss her. "I will never not love you," he added with a grin, taking advantage of the opportunity to use their new favorite word.

"What's wrong?" he asked, reacting to her sudden frown.

"It's Seth," she confided. "I'm worried about him."

Michael followed her gaze to the far corner of the garden where Seth stood alone.

"Go talk to him," he said, understanding her concern. "It's all right. I want to introduce Vincente and Maria to the rest of your family. You can catch up with us later."

"I love you," she said and kissed him tenderly.

"Hey," she said as she joined Seth where he stood with an empty champagne glass in hand. "Looks like you could use a refill."

She held up the bottle she'd lifted from the buffet table on the way over and handed it to him. "You pour.

"This is supposed to be a happy occasion," she teased when he'd filled both of their glasses.

He lifted his brows, managed a smile. "And are you happy?"

"I love him, Seth. And he loves me. So yes, I'm very happy."

He leaned forward, kissed her on the cheek. "Don't let it get away from you this time."

"I don't intend to. But right now I'm more concerned about you."

He lifted a shoulder, sipped champagne, stared at the garden without seeing.

"Am I going to have to bully it out of you?"

"Now there you go. Moving in on my territory. I'm the bully. You're the brat."

She smiled sadly and waited him out.

"I'm leaving town for a while," he said finally.

"Leaving? Seth—"

"Shh. I don't want the folks to know. If they get wind of it, they'll try to talk me out of going."

"Well, considering that *I* want to talk you out of go—"

"Tara, this is something I need to do, okay?"

Yes, she realized, it was something he needed to do. This business with his birth mother, Angie Donahue— the fact that she might have criminal ties as well as blood ties to the Kelley family—it had been eating him up inside.

"I wish there was something I could do to help," she said, feeling herself tearing up. "I wish—"

"I know," he said, cutting her off. "I know. And it helps. But this is something I have to do myself."

"Where will you go? How long are you going to be gone?"

"I don't know and I don't know."

"Well, that pins it down."

"I'll be okay," he insisted with a tight smile. "I've already worked things out at the law firm to take an indefinite leave. Just tell the folks not to worry and that I'll get in touch with them when I get settled."

"Now? You're leaving now?" she asked, reading the look in his eyes.

"Seems like as good a time as any." He set his glass on a table and pulled her into a warm embrace. "Be happy, brat."

"Call me? As soon as you—"

"I'll call, all right?" He touched a hand to her cheek. "I always loved you best, Terror."

She bit back tears for his sake. "I loved you better," she insisted, knowing he expected the competition, even now. And then she watched him walk away.

"He'll be okay, Tara," Michael said from behind her.

She turned into the arms he held out to her.

"He's a survivor."

Yes, she thought filled with love for this man who had survived so much to come back to her. They were all survivors, and she and Michael were proof that time, like love, can heal even the deepest wounds.

"Come on," he said gently. "We are suspiciously absent from our own party."

"Well," she said, shoring herself up on the love in his eyes, "what do you say, we remain suspiciously absent for, oh say, another thirty minutes or so?"

She took his hand, led him at a playful trot toward the maze beyond the garden.

"You're kidding," he said, even as she pulled him behind a carefully manicured hedge.

With a wicked smile, she reached up under her elegant ivory sheath and shimmied out of a pair of silk and lace panties.

She tossed them at him. He caught them on the fly.

"Would I kid about something like this?"

One side of his mouth kicked up in a totally male, totally intrigued grin. "Never," he said and dragged her against him.

"There's that word again."

And then there weren't any words—just two people hopelessly, helplessly in love, now, always, forever.

* * * * *

DYNASTIES: THE CONNELLYS

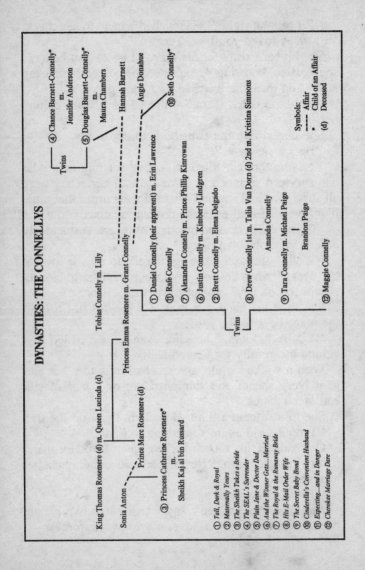

King Thomas Rosemere (d) m. Queen Lucinda (d)

Sonia Anton

Prince Marc Rosemere (d)

③ Princess Catherine Rosemere*
m.
Sheikh Kaj al bin Russard

Tobias Connelly m. Lilly

Princess Emma Rosemere m. Grant Connelly

④ Chance Barnett-Connelly*
m.
Jennifer Anderson

⑤ Douglas Barnett-Connelly*
m.
Maura Chambers

Twins

Hannah Barnett

Angie Donahue

⑩ Seth Connelly*

① Daniel Connelly (heir apparent) m. Erin Lawrence

⑪ Rafe Connelly

⑦ Alexandra Connelly m. Prince Phillip Kinrowan

④ Justin Connelly m. Kimberly Lindgren

② Brett Connelly m. Elena Delgado

⑧ Drew Connelly 1st m. Talia Van Dorn (d) 2nd m. Kristina Simmons

Amanda Connelly

⑨ Tara Connelly m. Michael Paige

Brandon Paige

⑫ Maggie Connelly

Twins

① *Tall, Dark & Royal*
② *Maternally Yours*
③ *The Sheikh Takes a Bride*
④ *The SEAL's Surrender*
⑤ *Plain Jane & Doctor Dad*
⑥ *And the Winner Gets...Married!*
⑦ *The Royal & the Runaway Bride*
⑧ *His E-Mail Order Wife*
⑨ *The Secret Baby Bond*
⑩ *Cinderella's Convenient Husband*
⑪ *Expecting...and in Danger*
⑫ *Cherokee Marriage Dare*

Symbols:
- - - - Affair
• Child of an Affair
(d) Deceased

DYNASTIES: THE CONNELLYS
continues...

Turn the page for a bonus look
at what's in store for you in the next
Connellys book
—only from Silhouette Desire!

CINDERELLA'S CONVENIENT
HUSBAND

by Katherine Garbera
October 2002

One

"What can I get for you?" asked the blond waitress.

Seth Connelly looked straight into eyes he'd never forgotten. They were the deep purple of crushed African violets. Lynn McCoy had been a troublemaking brat for the first five years of their acquaintance, then she'd blossomed into a beautiful young woman.

"Hello, Lynn," he said. Somehow when he'd thought of those he might see in Sagebrush, Montana, he'd forgotten about Lynn and that one awkward kiss they'd shared the night of her sixteenth birthday.

He'd never returned to the ranch again, aware that he'd crossed a line that shouldn't have been crossed. Aware that it was time to stop running and return home to Chicago.

But his birth mother's betrayal had made Chicago into a tense place, and he'd hit the road hoping to find some semblance of the man he'd become. Because as he'd fallen once again for Angie Donahue's lies and manipulation, he'd realized that he didn't know himself anymore.

He hoped Lynn didn't remember the embrace—it was so long ago. That one brief brush of lips still plagued his dreams on restless nights, because she had tasted innocent and he never had been.

Her eyes widened in recognition and she smiled at him. There was weariness on her face, and an instinctual part of him recognized that expression for what it was. She was running from something, as well.

Not your business, old man.

"Hi, Seth. What brings you to our little corner of the world?"

He couldn't tell her that he'd come here searching for something that he'd found in his youth. Something he couldn't really explain to anyone.

"I'm hoping for a cup of coffee and a steak."

"You've come to the right place. But I should tell you it's probably not as fancy as you'd get in Chicago."

"That's okay. The atmosphere's better here."

"Really? I'd have thought all those sophisticated people would win hands down."

"Nothing beats the mountains in Montana." Even though night had fallen, the view from the diner was one he'd never forgotten.

"You can say that again."

Here in this small town he wasn't the illegitimate son of a Mafia princess and Chicago's most-revered citizen. Here he was that wild boy who'd had his ear pierced and wore a leather jacket even in the heat of summer. Here he was a man without a family—and Seth needed that.

Lynn looked tired, he thought.

What kind of problems hung on her shoulders? Why wasn't Matt here, to relieve that burden for her?

What was Matt thinking to let his sister work in a

diner when there wasn't any reason for it? The McCoy spread was the biggest and most profitable in the area.

"Can you join me for a minute?"

"Just real quick."

"You're a hard worker, Lynn."

"Thank you," she said tentatively.

"Why the hesitation?"

"The last time you complimented me I found myself soaking wet on a cold evening."

"Hey, you're safe for now. I've grown into a boring old lawyer," he said.

"Not boring or old. Lawyer?"

"Okay, get it out of your system," he said.

"What?" she asked, all innocence. She looked breathtakingly lovely in the dim light of the diner.

"You've got to have a joke about lawyers."

"Not me. Besides I have nothing but respect for you," she said.

"Yeah, right. If memory serves, the last prank you played on me involved stealing my clothes and leaving me naked at the swimming hole."

"I left your hat, didn't I?"

He still felt a little embarrassed when he recalled the number of times she'd gotten the better of him. "I think we're square."

"I'm surprised you didn't call first."

"I didn't know I was coming until I got here."

She nodded. "I've got to get back to work. You take care, Seth Connelly."

She walked away and this time he watched and wanted. She was exactly as he remembered from that late summer night. Sweet and funny but tempered with the experiences life had used to test her. And he knew that it was probably for the best that Matt wasn't here and Seth would be moving on...again.

One

When Cutter Reno drifted out of Sundown, Montana, six years ago, he'd always figured he'd be back someday. He had friends here. He had memories here, some good, some not so good. And he supposed, in the overall scheme of things, Sundown came as close to "home" as any place he'd landed in his twenty-six years.

What he hadn't figured on was that when he did finally make an appearance it would be as the grand marshall of the annual Fourth of July parade.

Guess that goes to show how much he knew. He'd never counted on winning back-to-back National PRCA saddle bronc championships, either. And as it turned out, it was the celebrity status of the championships that had prompted his old buddy, Sam Perkins, to track him down and ask him to come back to lead the parade.

He shifted in the saddle and smiled at the faces lining

the street. Then he tried to think about the competitions and the money he was missing out on.

"Half the county will turn out to see you in the parade tomorrow," Sam had told him last night when they'd gotten together at the Dusk to Dawn Bar to catch up. "Why, it's downright huge."

By Sundown, Montana, population four hundred and seventy-three, standards, Cutter supposed it was a pretty big deal. Close as he could figure, it was four blocks long—a new record according to Sam—as it snaked with dogged enthusiasm along the length of Main Street strung with red, white and blue banners. Among the highlights was a twenty-one piece all-school marching band.

"Yeah, we'd a' had twenty-two marchers if Billy Capper hadn't busted his nose in the softball game yesterday when his face connected with Joe Gillman's bat." This from Snake Gibson, a barrel-chested old wrangler who'd joined in on the bull-slinging at the bar last night.

The consensus, over cold long necks and shelled peanuts, was that since Sundown had beaten neighboring Shueyville in a ninth inning squeaker, Billy's absence would be missed but not overly mourned.

The band seemed to be holding their own without him, too, Cutter thought, as they sweltered in their red wool uniforms, desperately tried to keep close ranks and belt out a Sousa march. It was a shame they were working so hard, though, because for all their efforts, he was a little embarrassed to discover that all eyes were turned on him.

Well, almost all eyes, Cutter conceded as he spotted a six-year-old memory that should have worked its way out of his system by now. The moment he saw Peg

Lathrop, Cutter lost all awareness of the summer sun beating down, burning through his gray-and-black plaid shirt.

The band, the laughter and the cheers from the crowd all faded to background noise as Cutter shifted to autopilot, automatically reining in the big bay gelding when it crow-hopped away from an escaped red balloon. He was only aware of the chestnut-haired woman who moved purposefully along the fringe of the route, avoiding his gaze like she was practicing a religion.

Pretty Peggy Lathrop. Man, Cutter thought as he watched her move along the parade route. She always had been a fine sight. Time had only improved on the package of sleek lines and knockout curves. Paint-tight blue jean cutoffs showed off slim hips and long tan legs. A tiny white spaghetti strap tank top hugged a pair of unbelievably lush breasts. The hint of a tanned tummy peeked between the scrap of stretchy cotton and the waistband of those hip-hugging shorts.

As his horse plodded along at parade speed, he did his damnedest to keep a bead on her. Beneath a pale straw Stetson that partially shaded her face, a length of satin straight hair fell to nearly her waist. The July sun glinted off the shining mass, setting off flashes of light like a prairie fire. When he finally got around to checking out the face her hat brim shadowed, he was just as taken as he was with the rest of her—and got pleasantly lost in a sweet summer memory of long-legged Peg.

Never taking his eyes off her, he lifted his hat, resettled it, and with a smile of pure pleasure, prepared to get sentimentally sappy over the fire of an old flame that had never quite burned itself out. They'd had a little thing six years ago. It had been the summer of his sophomore year in the PRCA. He'd been flying high still pumped up over being named Rookie of the Year. He'd come home to Sundown a hero then, too. And he'd found little Peg all grown up. When he left town again, he'd left a winner in more ways than one.

Still watching her, he shifted the reins to his left hand, absently rubbed the flat of his palm along his thigh. There was no way that she didn't remember. He'd seen it in her eyes in that brief moment when their gazes had connected over the crowd. He'd waited for her to smile for him. Instead, she'd looked away faster than the swish of the gelding's tail.

He was still looking, though. He may have been too busy the past few years for more than fleeting thoughts of those hot summer nights they'd spent together, but he hadn't forgotten. Dew damp grass. Round July moon. Soft, surrendering sighs. Seeing her again brought all those memories front and center. She'd had an innocence about her back then that had just tangled him up inside, a lack of inhibition that had made him drunk with lust. The taste of her. The sweet, giving heat. *Man, had there been heat.* Enough heat that just seeing her again made him wonder what pretty Peggy was up to these days.

"Cutter—hey Cutter, over here!"

He whipped his head around, a winning smile in place as a dozen cameras clicked. He tipped his hat to a little cowboy in tall boots and a big hat who was grinning up at him from the curb as if Cutter held the key to Candyland.

Peg hadn't smiled at him that way. Peg hadn't smiled at him at all. Her pretty brown eyes had looked right past him while he was still recovering from the punch of pure, spontaneous arousal that had bolted through his body like a summer lightning strike. All flash and fire and electricity.

No. She hadn't smiled. He didn't know quite what to make of that. Most women did a lot more than smile for him. Peg had done a *whole* lot more six years ago. They'd had a good time. At least *he* had. From all indications, she had, too. He didn't know if her not smiling for him made him feel bad, or mad or just plain puzzled.

Cutter got a line on Peg's straw hat again as she moved easily among the crowd. He caught the smile she gave to a pretty redhead about her age. Scowled as she showed her pearly whites to a gaggle of ranch hands who gaped in awe then panted and groaned in ecstasy as she passed them by.

The booming crack of a cherry bomb sent the bay into a skittering dance that ended up with him snorting and raring on his hind legs and striking at the air. Cutter settled him with a soft murmur and a strong hand that had the crowd *ahing* in approval just as the band broke into a rousing country rendition of "God Bless the U.S.A."

When Cutter looked around, Peg was gone…without a smile—which, he'd decided, he was going to get from pretty Peggy before he blew back out of town tomorrow.

Everybody smiled for Cutter Reno. Everybody.

Silhouette Desire

presents

DYNASTIES: THE CONNELLYS

A brand-new miniseries about the Connellys of Chicago,
a wealthy, powerful American family tied by blood to the
royal family of the island kingdom of Altaria.
They're wealthy, powerful and rocked by
scandal, betrayal...and passion!

Look for a whole year of glamorous and
utterly romantic tales in 2002:

January: **TALL, DARK & ROYAL by Leanne Banks**

February: **MATERNALLY YOURS by Kathie DeNosky**

March: **THE SHEIKH TAKES A BRIDE by Caroline Cross**

April: **THE SEAL'S SURRENDER by Maureen Child**

May: **PLAIN JANE & DOCTOR DAD by Kate Little**

June: **AND THE WINNER GETS...MARRIED! by Metsy Hingle**

July: **THE ROYAL & THE RUNAWAY BRIDE by Kathryn Jensen**

August: **HIS E-MAIL ORDER WIFE by Kristi Gold**

September: **THE SECRET BABY BOND by Cindy Gerard**

October: **CINDERELLA'S CONVENIENT HUSBAND
by Katherine Garbera**

November: **EXPECTING...AND IN DANGER by Eileen Wilks**

December: **CHEROKEE MARRIAGE DARE
by Sheri WhiteFeather**

Silhouette

Where love comes alive™

Visit Silhouette at www.eHarlequin.com   SDDYN02

If you enjoyed what you just read,
then we've got an offer you can't resist!

Take 2 bestselling love stories FREE!

Plus get a FREE surprise gift!

COMING NEXT MONTH

#1465 TAMING THE OUTLAW—Cindy Gerard

After six years, sexy Cutter Reno was back in town and wreaking havoc on Peg Lathrop's emotions. Peg still yearned passionately for Cutter—and he wanted to pick up where they had left off. But would he still want her once he learned her precious secret?

#1466 CINDERELLA'S CONVENIENT HUSBAND—Katherine Garbera

Dynasties: The Connellys

Lynn McCoy would do anything to keep the ranch that had been in her family for generations—even marry wealthy Seth Connelly. And when she fell in love with him, Lynn needed to convince her handsome husband they could have their very own happily-ever-after.

#1467 THE SEAL's SURPRISE BABY—Amy J. Fetzer

A trip home turned Jack Singer's life upside down because he learned that beautiful Melanie Patterson, with whom he'd spent one unforgettable night, had secretly borne him a daughter. The honor-bound Navy SEAL proposed a marriage of convenience. But Melanie refused, saying she didn't want him to feel obligated to her. Could Jack persuade her he wanted to be a *real* father...and husband?

#1468 THE ROYAL TREATMENT—Maureen Child

Crown and Glory

Determined to get an interview with the royal family, anchorwoman Jade Erickson went to the palace—and found herself trapped in an elevator in the arms of the handsomest man she'd ever seen. Jeremy Wainwright made her heart beat faster, and he was equally attracted to her, but would the flame of their unexpected passion continue to burn red-hot?

#1469 HEARTS ARE WILD—Laura Wright

Maggie Connor got more than she'd bargained for when she vowed to find the perfect woman for her very attractive male roommate. Nick Kaplan was turning out to be everything *she'd* ever wanted in a man, and she was soon yearning to keep him for herself!

#1470 SECRETS, LIES...AND PASSION—Linda Conrad

An old flame roared back to life when FBI agent Reid Sorrels returned to his hometown to track a suspect. His former fiancée, Jill Bennett, was as lovely as ever, and the electricity between them was undeniable. But they both had secrets....

SDCNM0902